To: my foxhunting sister Jane,
Happy Birthday!
Love,
Sara

3

"The little brown mare went down to the branch with her head loose."

THE DERRYDALE PRESS
FOXHUNTERS' LIBRARY

The
SILVER HORN

And Other Sporting Tales of John Weatherford

GORDON GRAND

THE DERRYDALE PRESS
LANHAM AND NEW YORK

THE DERRYDALE PRESS

Published in the United States of America
by The Derrydale Press
4720 Boston Way, Lanham, Maryland 20706

Distributed by NATIONAL BOOK NETWORK, INC.

British Library Cataloguing in Publication Information Available

Library of Congress Cataloging-in-Publication Data

Grand, Gordon.
  The silver horn and other sporting tales of John Weatherford / Gordon
Grand.
      p.   cm.
    ISBN 1-58667-039-5 (cloth : alk. paper)—ISBN 1-56416-190-0 (leather-
bound : alk. paper)
    1. Horses—Anecdotes. 2.Fox hunting—anecdotes. I. Title.

SF301 .G7 2000
636.1—dc21   00-060333

♾™The paper used in this publication meets the minimum requirements of
American National Standard for Information Sciences—Permanence of
Paper for Printed Library Materials, ANSI/NISO Z39.48-1992.
Manufactured in the United States of America.

TO

E. D. G.

"When we asked concerning her
the plowman said
'She be way way forrard with hounds
— a days furrows forrard.'"

Contents

Illustrations

The Silver Horn

CHAPTER I.

John Weatherford, Sportsman

MANY stout foxes have been hunted and accounted for
since these slim little stories reminiscent of my friend, Colonel John Weatherford, were written. The Colonel has now
joined the goodly company of sportsmen of the past, and if
there is a communion of Masters of Fox Hounds I venture
to think he is sitting at their high table.

Those of his more scholarly friends who had no contact
with him as a sportsman may resent the publishing of these
stories on the ground that they picture him only in the pursuit of pleasure, and as one having no serious purpose in life.
My answer is that a comprehensive portrait of the man must
wait upon a more erudite pen than mine, for his interests
and activities were manifold.

It may add to the reader's interest in the stories to know
who and of what manner of man the Colonel was.

He was descended from that John Fortesque Weatherford who came to this country from Weatherford Combe,
Devonshire, in 1673 and settled in the Massachusetts Bay
Colony, where the family furnished its quota of early governors, soldiers, merchant philanthropists and members of
the judiciary.

The feats at arms of Colonel Ezra Weatherford of Revolutionary fame (affectionately known as "Old Long Arms") are matters of history, and readers of Parkman will recall the adroit treaty which Captain Grenville Weatherford negotiated single-handed with that perpetual trouble-maker, Chief Aquossoc, which brought peace to the struggling Colony. The lucid diction and sound reasoning of Justice John Kingsley Weatherford's Opinions are quoted to this day by the judiciary and bar of the Commonwealth of Massachusetts and are still held to be good law.

But it was chiefly in the realm of commerce and as ship owners that the family made its impress on the young New England States; Richard Perkins' book on the Weatherford Clipper Fleet is well known to all New Englanders with nautical backgrounds.

My old friend was the son of the late James Fortesque Weatherford, whose acumen, integrity and public spiritedness are still bywords among the older banking fraternity of Boston.

Inheriting a comfortable fortune, which he substantially augmented, John Weatherford retired early from all business associations and devoted much of his time and patrimony to archaeological researches directed to broadening our common knowledge of Greek culture. My interest in him in connection with this book is only as a sportsman.

He was an impressive figure of a man, standing an inch or two over six feet and of a powerful physique. Older Harvard men will recall him as an oarsman of whom I have heard it said there was no finer.

A natural aptitude for sport coupled with abundant means and leisure made him an adept with rod and gun.

For forty years he controlled one of the prime duck-shooting properties on the Atlantic seaboard, and an extensive quail property in South Carolina, and with three associates held a lease from the Canadian Government on a stretch of salmon water that excelled any I have yet fished. He was the best man in a woodcock cover with whom I ever shot. In piecing together these stories having chiefly to do with horses and hunting I have often been tempted to wander and tell of days in which my diary abounds, of the Colonel in his shooting jacket.

Of the one phase of sport which probably held the greatest interest for him I know practically nothing, his breeding of thoroughbred horses. He was unalterably opposed to publicity and never appeared as the owner or breeder of a race horse, other than timber horses, nor was he prone to discuss his breeding activities with his intimates. All I ever knew was that he owned about a dozen of the most fashionably bred and highly proved matrons, and studied exhaustively the problems of their mating. What mares they were or how they were bred I never knew. They were kept for him by various friends in Virginia and Kentucky, but how the business was handled was a closed book. What I do know is that one of the most knowledgeable and widely known breeders in the country once said to me that if the history of the American thoroughbred was ever written truly, the name of John Weatherford would be spread large on its pages; from which I judged that the Colonel must have produced some very noteworthy race horses with which his name has never been associated.

I now come to the man himself. We were friends and neighbors for twenty-odd years, and I had countless opportunities of observing him in the major and minor situations of life; he will ever stand out in my memory as the kindliest of men. He was generous, sympathetic and intuitively just.

Those who were most constantly with him — his servants, his dogs and his horses — gave him freely of their best and were devoted to him. At the time of his death there were said to be twenty-odd of his employees, either active or retired, who had been in his service over thirty years. They included gamekeepers, sailors, stable men, gardeners, etc., for all of whom ample provision had been made.

He was never known to sell a horse which had carried him well, saying to me many times that he could not tolerate the thought of such a hunting companion falling upon evil days.

I once saw him pay a woman $1500 for a brave, courageous, but undersized little horse not worth half that amount, because it distressed him to see the horse's mouth grabbed every time he landed over a fence. On the day in question the Colonel turned just in time to see the horse crucified in mid-air over a formidable chicken coop and hook its hocks on the top of the coop so that its legs bled. I can see the Colonel's face now as he said to me, "I have watched that going on for two seasons. It spoils my sport," and with that he went up and bought the horse, which he had heard was for sale, and gave it to our Scotch doctor's little girl, who was a finished rider.

He once presented a sensitive bird dog of which he was fond to a cousin, and upon hearing that the man was sharp of temper with his dogs, sent his car three hundred and fifty miles to bring the dog home and paid a famous handler in North Carolina $300 to supply the cousin with another dog.

I mention these incidents in the belief that they portray the Colonel better than any words of eulogy.

That it may not be said that this sketch fails to recognize

traits which offended certain people, it is admitted that at times the Colonel appeared a bit overbearing and overdetermined to have his own way. It is also true that he was not a placid person with whom to ride when hounds were boiling along. He rode hard and straight and with a never-faltering determination to stay with hounds. In the accomplishment of this he would sometimes bustle along seemingly regardless of others yet it was only the weak and timid riders who took offense. The first-flight brigade welcomed his challenges and enjoyed having it out with him.

He had small patience with the lowering of rails when hounds were running and when his progress was arrested by a group of less bold riders halting to dislodge a top rail his language could be very virile. When once over a fence however, he would be the first to risk losing a run by catching a horse for one of those very same obstructionists.

The Colonel was under no illusion respecting the good or bad qualities of his own horses, dogs, yachts, guns or whatever it might be, and was correspondingly outspoken regarding your possessions. There were those who resented this frankness. If you were unfortunate enough to have bought a narrow-waisted horse, through being deceived by a superabundance of present fat, the Colonel would take one penetrating look at the horse and tell you in no uncertain language that you should have known better than to have bought such an animal; that it would never stand work; that it had no place in which to store its dinner and that at the end of a fortnight's work a garter would suffice to span it. When a strong character possesses tact we classify him as a potential statesman. Lacking tact we say he is brusque.

We of today are trustees for one of the world's most

priceless possessions, regard for the unwritten roll of "the things no fellow does." This list has come down to us as a heritage from the sportsmen of all the ages, and when our course is run it will be our bounden duty to bequeath it to the oncoming generation inviolate. There was no man of my time who more conscientiously preserved this heritage than did John Weatherford.

ARTHUR PENDLETON.

CHAPTER II.

The Silver Horn

O N A sparkling summer morning in early September I was breakfasting under the fine old gnarled apple tree that stands off the corner of my house. I was in a tingling, buoyant state and well I might be for we had had a rare cubbing morning and many pleasant things had contributed to my well-being since my return, and other pleasant things were in the immediate offing. Those that had happened included a swim in the pool, the feel of a fresh pongee suit, the taste of an iced cantaloupe, and a first cup of coffee. Those in the offing were two boiled eggs whose natal day I could vouch for, three slices of crisp bacon, a second cup of coffee, a smoke, and the morning paper.

I was in the act of pouring the second cup of coffee when the morning mail was placed on the table. The mail had no interest for me until I noticed a generous envelope postmarked London and addressed in Colonel John Weatherford's handwriting.

When I had finished breakfast I lit a cigarette, took my coffee and the letter over to a comfortable lounge chair, opened the letter and read:

Dear Pendleton:

I had a delightful chance meeting with Florence in London

the other morning. The enclosed tells the story. "Good hunting" to you. I will be home soon.

Faithfully,

J. W.

THE SILVER HORN

A nocturne of old London town

I said to the head waiter of that venerable hotel on Albemarle street, "Make my compliments to the lady who has just come in to breakfast and is sitting over in the corner and say I very particularly commend broiled finnan haddie."

The pompous and ponderous dignitary returned a moment later. "The lady is much obliged, Sir, but told me to say, Sir, that she has quite a different idea about her breakfast. Quite different, if I might say so, Sir — thank you, Sir — and the lady says, Sir, as how she would be obliged if you would stop and speak with her on your way out, Sir."

When I had finished my own finnan haddie, I stopped to wish Florence "the top of the morning."

"A man who will eat finnan haddie," she said mysteriously, "doesn't deserve to hear hunting horns under a summer moon."

"What do you mean?" I asked.

"Didn't you hear him?"

"Hear whom?"

"The lone huntsman of Albemarle street?"

"No, my rooms are on the Dover street side."

"Oh," said Florence, "what bad luck! You missed the most delightful thing." And then she told me this story:

[8]

Returning from the theater and supper she had drifted off into a sound sleep, from which she was gently and fancifully awakened without sensing the cause. Her watch showed three o'clock. The roar and rumble of London had faded to its lowest murmur. A midsummer moon filtered through and illuminated the street below. What was it that had so illusively awakened the sleeper? Again she listened. The faint mellow note of a hunting horn drifted up from Piccadilly.

Now a hunting horn is one thing to some people, and a very different thing to some other people. In Mrs. Grundy's family it represents only a noise; in Florence's family and to Florence herself it is a mystic spring which unlocks myriad memories and pictures; so at 3 a.m. Florence was hanging far out of a front window of her hotel, her eyes searching the moonlit London street.

A solitary figure was strolling at his leisure up the center of the street. To the tutored eye of the lady of the balcony, there was the slightest tinge of a roll to his gait. There is much of romance in Florence, and her coffee grew colder and colder as the description ran on. The gleam of his white waistcoat, the cut of his dress coat, the sheen of his silk hat worn just a bit toward the back of the head, the cane hooked over his left arm, and — touch of touches — the gleam of a silver horn tucked between the white tie and top shirt stud. "Mind you," said Florence, "just exactly where a huntsman would carry it. Oh, it was too delicious." Well, this reveler of the night halted in front of Florence's window. Why just there, I did not inquire, but Florence had said she was hanging out of the window.

With feet far apart and leaning back on his cane, the gentle reveler plucked forth his horn, and made old Albemarle street resound. Twang. Twang. Twang. Then he warmed to his task. "Hoick, Hoick! Furrier has it. Hoick! For'ard to Furrier! Hold hard, gentlemen! Hold hard, please! Ah, Rattler Boy. Hoick! For'ard to Furrier! Steady, gentlemen, please. Let hounds get out of covert. Let them get straightened away. Please don't press hounds." And then, in a glorious, resounding voice that rolled on from street to street, "Gone away — gone away — Hoick! For'ard!" After three more sharp notes of the horn indicating that hounds had found and gone away, and as a signal and final exhortation to any hounds that might be left in covert, the horn was once more inserted between the white tie and top shirt stud.

The lone Huntsman, cheering and encouraging his hounds, passed on toward Grafton street. Hounds ran a burning line with fine head up Albemarle street, but at The Royal Institute they dwelled on the line and faulted.

The Huntsman cast them up the noble steps of the Institute and then in a narrow service alley at the Piccadilly side of the building. In the alley he was met by the bewildered guardian hurrying out to see what the hue and cry might be.

"Hold hard, Sir. Dash it, Sir! Don't you see hounds are casting? You will have their heads up in a minute. Hold hard!"

Then Furrier opened, the pack honored, and away they flew toward Grafton street. Of course, Albemarle street ends at Grafton, and there was a great to-do as to whether the fox had turned right-handed to Old Bond street or left-handed to Dover street. Again hounds faulted and up went their heads. Again the twang of the horn calling hounds to him, and then patiently he cast a little way toward Old Bond — then a little toward Dover — and finally a bit back on Albemarle. On this latter cast he encountered the old guardian of the venerable Institute standing in the middle of the road, his eyes agog.

"That's right, my man, that's right. Never fuss about when hounds are at fault."

"Of course, I think he should have cast first toward Dover street," said Florence, "because the breeze was blowing toward Hyde Park corner."

Then he cast them up on to the porch of Quaritch's, that great book shop on Grafton street, into Bunting's, the bootmaker's on Dover, and even as far back as Boss's, the master gunmaker's shop on Albemarle, probably thinking that the fox might have been turned at the Institute and headed back toward Piccadilly.

At last the riddle was solved. The true line ran toward Dover street and so down Little Hay Hill where Huntsman and horn drifted out of hearing; but Florence said she heard the horn once more across Berkeley Square and about opposite Dartmouth House on Charles street. She said she then went to bed and to sleep, but I rather think she fell to romancing.

When Florence told me this tale, and I thought of those hounds of the imagination casting for the line around Quaritch's, I could but wonder what all the old English worthies depicted in word and illustration in Quaritch's first editions would have thought of that young English blade of this year of grace alone at three o'clock in the morning hunting his hounds in the heart of moonlit old London town. I do believe that there must have been many a good British sportsman tucked away in his bed close to the line of the hunted fox that night, whose heart beat a bit faster as he listened to the twang of that horn and the cheery "Hoick! For'ard!" and those

THE SILVER HORN

who had long since resigned from the pigskin must have had mellow memories of their own youth awakened.

When I stopped at the mail desk, a ruby-faced old gentleman was saying to the mail clerk, "I say, what a go that young chap was having last night — splendid voice for a huntsman — splendid! Reminded me of my days with the Earl of Fitzwilliams' hounds. When I heard him turn down Little Hay Hill I said to myself, 'Ah, now there's a sweet stretch to watch hounds race down.' Blest if I could get back to sleep for an hour. Of course, I thought it a bit nervy to call his hound Furrier, after George Osbaldeston's great hound, but it might jolly well be that he thought he was the Squire or old Meynell. Oh, youth — that's the thing — youth! When you get to be my age it's a grand thing to know that you made good use of it."

The old gentleman pulled on his gloves, squared his shoulders, slipped his stick on his arm, and marched off, looking, I thought, very fit.

CHAPTER III.

Major Denning's Trust Estate

I ENTERTAIN no grievances of a personal nature against the barbers of New London, Marblehead or even Nantucket. I concede that the patrons of these several artists may think highly of them and with just cause, but the fact remains that when, on my month's cruise, I entered the harbors of these respective places determined upon having my hair cut I invariably weakened and argued myself into remaining unshorn pending my return to our own village barber.

It is a very pleasant place, this shop of Antonio Spinnello's, with its four bird cages painted a Venetian red and little brass urns at the top of them, and the shelves under the windows aglow with gaily painted pots filled with a bewildering array of flowers. It was, therefore, with fine satisfaction that I settled down in Antonio's familiar red plush chair to listen to all that had happened in our village during my absence. Antonio was warming to his task of historian.

"Mrs. Madden, the huntsman's wife. She haffa new ba-beé. a girl ba-beé — not so good — eh! She makea the ninea one. By gol. Ninea ba-beés. The Colonel Weatherford — heem away — alla time he go away, but before he go he geeve Mrs. Madden the ten dollar gold, but he say, 'Now, Mrs. Madden — by gol you are careful it be a boy ba-beé thisa time.' That a good joke on the beeg Colonel. The ten dollar — she all gone and another girl ba-beé."

Just then I heard the door open and saw the figure of a tall, distinguished looking man with white hair and a small white goatee reflected in the glass. He was dressed in black and wore a large soft hat of a kind seldom seen north of Mason and Dixon's Line. He stepped up to Antonio, and said with a soft Kentucky drawl, "If I could interrupt you, Suh, might I leave my razors to be attended to, and Mr. Spinnello, Suh, will you do me the kindness of giving 'Tuesday' your best attention? It has never given me the same service as its associates. When may I call for them, Suh?" "In the morning. I have them fixed up good," said Antonio, and the old gentleman departed.

I looked at Antonio in the glass. His face bore a reverent expression as he gazed at a set of seven small English razors in a pigskin case polished by years of use. Each razor rested in a groove lined with crimson velvet. "Look," said Antonio, and he handed me one of the razors with "Tuesday" and the name, "Dulaney Denning," engraved on the back. "Antonio," I said, "who is that old gentleman?" "By gol, you don't know? Ah, you haff been away. You do not know. He ees Major Denning. You go way — he come. By gol. A fine gentleman. He leef at Mrs. Martan's. One-half of the ground floor all fixed up new for heem. Living room here — bedroom — there — bathroom, all new — here. The Major — where he come from — who he ees, by gol I don't know."

A day or two later I was in Mr. Maloney's general store getting six bags of cattle salt. As Mr. Maloney's man was storing the salt in the back of my Ford station wagon the old gentleman I had seen in the barber shop came into the store followed by a small bare-footed colored boy carrying a basket.

"Mr. Maloney, Suh," said the old gentleman, "I hope I find you well. Will you favor me, Suh, with two of your best oranges, and a quarter of a pound of that excellent cheese of yours. How much, Suh, will discharge my indebtedness?"

"Ephraim, pay Mr. Maloney and put my provisions in the basket," upon which Ephraim took a coin from his pocket and handed it to Mr. Maloney.

Major Denning then turned to Mr. Maloney and said, "My friend, Doctor McTavish, tells me that Mrs. Maloney is indisposed. I pray, Suh, it is not of a serious nature, and that you will commend me to your lady." And the old gentleman walked out of the store followed by his diminutive servant.

Mr. Maloney turned to me and said in his up-State accent, "I declare to goodness, Mr. Pendleton, if it ain't a pleasure to have that old gentleman come inside of this store. Dang it, if he don't make me feel like I owned a thousand acres of land. That's Hattie Jackson's boy he has a-following of him. He comes in here most every morning, and spends mebbe fifteen cents but I cal'ate I'd rather see him walk in here than some what spends two dollars. 'I pray, Suh, that you will commend me to your lady' — did you hear him say that to me? And he don't just say it. No sir. He means it. Why Mrs. Martin where he lives told my daughter-in-law that it don't make no difference how many times a day he sees her working about he just natur'ly bows to her like he hadn't seen her for a month."

On the following Saturday I was exhibiting some of my Aberdeen Angus cattle at the Valley Fair. In the afternoon I climbed up to the top row of the grandstand to watch the trotting races. It was a scorching day. As the first heat was about to start, who did I see climbing up towards the top of the stand, followed by his colored boy, but Major Denning.

Upon reaching the second row from the top he instructed the boy to open a colossal black cotton umbrella and to sit on the seat behind him and hold the umbrella over him. Thus comfortably ensconced he settled down to enjoy the sport. I then took it upon myself to go over to him, introduce myself, and sit down beside him. It was under such circumstances that a valued friendship had its inception.

Our conversation seemed to drift naturally towards horses, and no one whom I had met, not even Colonel Weatherford himself, had such a fund of information respecting blood lines. Of the trotter he knew absolutely nothing, but he was keenly interested in the races simply because they were races. Apparently there was nothing in the realm of sport or competitive games which did not interest him. He said to me, "Mr. Pendelton, Suh, a competition between two hound puppies contending with vigor for the same bone quickens my pulse."

Nothing would satisfy the Major short of my sitting under the umbrella with him. Now I hold a minor political post in our county and the grandstand was crowded with my country constituents whom I knew would not take kindly to seeing one of their elective officers shielded from the sun by the labors of a free born American citizen. Nevertheless, I sat under the umbrella and appreciated it.

As the sun began to dip behind us the Major instructed Ephraim to tilt the umbrella backwards in order to keep the sun from our backs and necks. This new position of the umbrella obliterated the entire track from Ephraim's vision, and so at the finish of each heat the old gentleman would report, "Ephraim, the sorrel horse won," or "the black mare won," upon which Ephraim who had never at any time seen either horse would say, "Yas, Sah, Mr. Major, yas, Sah."

Between one of the races the Major asked me if I happened to know Colonel Weatherford. Upon my telling him that I did he exclaimed, "It has been my privilege, Suh, to number Colonel Weatherford among my friends for forty years. I rank him, Suh, as the first gentleman, the very first, among my acquaintances. I come from that part of Kentucky where every gentleman is a horseman, and Kentucky would be proud to boast of Colonel Weatherford as one of her sons. He does me the honor of serving as one of the trustees of my trust estate — The Dulaney Denning Trust Estate. The other trustee is my friend, Mr. James H. Parkins of the Drovers Loan and Trust Company in New York City — a very fine Northern gentleman, and it pleases me to think that his bank is one of the soundest in the country, so I have no apprehension, none whatsoever, concerning my trust estate." This was my introduction to the Dulaney Denning Trust Estate. When the races were over we parted, but with a promise on my part to call on him the next afternoon at five o'clock to partake of a mint julep.

The Widow Martin, an estimable woman in frugal circumstances, lived in a small, white house on one of our lesser side streets. As Antonio Spinnello had said, one-half of the first floor of her house had been converted into an apartment for the Major; it consisted of a diminutive living room, bedroom and bath. The place was furnished only with what Mrs. Martin had been able to spare, but it had that rare atmosphere of homeiness which invites one to stay and visit. The pictures themselves were worth a long trip to see, for the walls were literally covered with photos and paintings of famous race horses of the past.

It has been my privilege to witness the ceremony of con- cocting and serving mint juleps conducted by a number of Kentucky gentlemen of the old school, but never have I seen the event solemnized with greater nicety and punctiliousness than Major Dulaney Denning put into it that day.

Since my first introduction to Ephraim he had been equipped with shoes, and had apparently been rigorously schooled in his part of this rite of hospitality, for he waited upon his master hand and foot. It struck me as a coincidence that the Bourbon was of the same brand and bottling as fa- vored by Colonel Weatherford. The day being warm the frosting on the two old George III silver goblets was well- nigh perfect. When all had been done to the Major's liking he came over and sat down, upon which Ephraim placed the juleps on an eighteenth century silver tray of beautiful de- sign and proportions and passed them with all the ceremony of an ancient body servant. This accomplished, he offered thin slices from the quarter of a pound of Mr. Maloney's "most excellent cheese." I determined there and then that we in the North offered but meagre hospitality when we simply pressed a button and ordered cocktails to be made. This was the first of many mint juleps I enjoyed in that snug living room, and the first of many long talks from which I derived much that has stood me in good stead. I learned of some fine, enjoyable things that life had to offer which were in no way dependent upon material possessions.

The Major stayed with us for five years and the old gen- tleman made a life-long impress on the memories of all who came in contact with him. There are those who will tell you, as will Mr. Maloney and his lady, that Major Denning improved the hearts and manners of our whole village, and perhaps he did. We knew comparatively little about him, but we did know that he came from a family long famous in Kentucky as breeders of thoroughbreds, and that the Major was accredited with being one of the best versed men in that State in the breeding, raising, training and racing of horses. We also gathered that he had been a confirmed and inveterate gambler, and had completely dissipated a fine old property through this ungovernable passion.

He eschewed all social contact with us and nothing could persuade him to enter my house, nor did I ever meet him any place in town except at Colonel Weatherford's. I ascribed this to the fact that he could not repay hospitality in kind; also he had no means of transportation and was sensitive about being sent for. There was, however, never a sporting event within a radius of twenty-five miles that he did not find ways and means of attending.

In respect to sport he had true Anglo-Saxon adaptability. As he was barred from his life-long association with thoroughbred horses and the track, he took to a secondary love, and went shooting on every possible occasion. He soon became the boon companion of those who shot, and was ever ready on an hour's notice to shoot duck, quail, woodcock, pheasant or rabbits with any one who would favor him with a lift to the shooting country. As he was an excellent shot, the best of company and possessed of two priceless dogs given him by Colonel Weatherford, the barrels of his gun were often warm. The state of excitement into which our old Scotch doctor, Donald McTavish, and the Major would work themselves when the woodcock flight was on, was a rebuke to some of us, for the doctor was seventy-three and the Major seventy-seven.

One of the mysteries surrounding this delightful character was his famous Trust Estate. He received his funds once a month from that grandfather of institutions, the Drovers Loan and Trust Company in New York. I say he received it from the Trust Company. This is hardly correct for it came to him direct from James H. Parkins, the President. For reasons best known to the trustees the money due Mrs. Martin for the apartment was always paid to her direct. This, said the Major, was to save him the burden of handling Mrs. Martin's money. I wondered. The amount turned over to the Major appeared to be the minimum with which a person could keep supplied with oranges, cheese and tobacco. Even the laundry bills were discharged through Mrs. Martin.

On or about May and October 1st of each year it was understood that the Major would require a new suit and on these occasions he would address himself to the trustees inquiring into the then condition of his trust estate. These letters were couched, as were all his contacts, in the most gallant and courteous terms. In a spirit of pride in his trust estate he once read me a letter he had just composed to the trustees. It read as follows:

James H. Parkins and John Weatherford, Esquires,
Co-Trustees of the Dulaney Denning Trust Estate,
New York City.
Gentlemen:

I preface with my compliments and expressions of regard. The comments in the public press telling of the continuing satisfactory condition of our country augur well for the security of my trust estate.

In spite, however, of the present sound state of affairs, I urge a continuation of the greatest conservatism in the selection of investments for my trust estate, and beg that you will not be tempted or misled by the blandishments of any of those plausible young men who advocate the purchase of mining or oil stocks, nor even those who entertain the highest possible hope for the future of shares whose prosperity depends upon the public's acceptance of patented cream separators or domestic articles of any kind. Over a period of fifty years I have discovered that even the most courteous of these young men are often misled.

I have occasion, gentlemen, to address you upon a matter of moment. I have had under advisement the replenishment of my wardrobe.

Prior to having my tailor wait upon me I wish to inquire upon what surplus I may count in my trust estate for this purpose.

I remain, gentlemen, with renewed expressions of regard,
Very faithfully yours,
DULANEY DENNING.

Meeting the Major at the post office a few days hence, nothing would do but I must read the reply to this letter.

Major Dulaney Denning,
Dear Major Denning:

This will acknowledge your letter of May 23rd. I am glad to confirm your opinion regarding the present satisfactory condition of your trust estate.

Regarding your sartorial requirements. You once very

sagely remarked that eternal vigilance was the handmaiden of financial security. I have reviewed your trust estate and might I suggest, my dear Major, the purchase of but one suit at this time?

I have today requested Messrs. Simpson & Walker who have served Colonel Weatherford for close to fifty years, and who have your measurements, to forward you a comprehensive assortment of samples, and have arranged with them to send me their bill covering the one suit. Through thus limiting your purchases, there will be no impairment of the capital of your trust estate.

As it is approximately the first of the month I enclose a check for $25.00 for the usual special purpose.

Faithfully,

James H. Parkins.

"There," said the Major, "that is the sort of trust estate to have," and put the letter back in his inside pocket. He started to move away, but returned and said, "I would not wish you to think, Suh, that there was anything peculiar or unusual about the money sent for the special purpose. Quite the contrary, Suh. My trustees simply recognize that all gentlemen must maintain their interest in the racing of horses just as they maintain their religious observances, and so I receive this special distribution from the Estate of $25 per month, which I may venture upon horses of my choice. But I regret to observe, Mr. Pendleton, that there is much amiss in the method of conducting racing today, for it is evident from my own experience that the best horses seldom win." As I climbed into my car I could but think that the Dulaney Denning Trust Estate was a very unusual institution.

Something over four years rolled by when of a sudden strange events began to take place.

Colonel Weatherford said to me one day, "What do you know and hear about Denning these days. Mrs. Martin wrote me last week that he has recently taken to staying away for days at a time, a thing he has never done before."

A week later I was standing on the steps of our bank talking to the Colonel when he took my arm and said, "Look." I looked and there driving up the village street paying not the slightest regard to our one traffic light of which we are proud, was the Major, in a new shiny car. "Come with me," said the Colonel, and we crossed the street to the agency of that particular car and learned that they had just sold the Major a car. "Is it paid for?" asked the Colonel in a somewhat anxious voice. "Oh yes," said the agent. "The Major gave us a check on our own local bank." We re-crossed the street to the bank of which the Colonel was a director and member of the executive committee. He disappeared into the bank, returning in about two minutes with the illuminating expression, "Well, I'll be d———d."

It was then about luncheon time so the Colonel suggested that we lunch at his house. We had no sooner sat down at the table than the 'phone rang and Albert came in to give the Colonel a message. His face clouded over and he said: "Thank her and say I am obliged for the information." He looked glum for a moment, then his annoyance passed off and he said to me with a smile, "That was Jim Parkins' secretary. She said Mr. Parkins wants to know whether I had noticed in the report of the sale at Belmont Park yesterday that Major Denning had bought a horse for $350. Pendleton, when a thing is born in the blood it is certainly there for all time."

He sent for Albert, requisitioned the morning paper, and there, in an account of a sale of horses in training, was the notation of the sale of the chestnut three-year-old colt, *Eternal Hope* by *Eternal* out of *Maid of Hope*, $350, Dulaney Denning, buyer.

As I was about to leave the house the Colonel said, "Have you any plans which will take you to the track?" "No" I answered, "but I would not mind a day's racing on Saturday." "Well," said the Colonel, "if you get a chance, see what you can you find out about this *Eternal* colt."

Between the second and third race on Saturday I ran into Jim Andrews, for whom I had been looking all afternoon. Andrews had trained a horse or two for me at one time to our mutual profit and we were fast friends. There is no one's opinion respecting a horse I would rather have than Jim Andrews'. "Jim," I said, "I want to see you. I want your best opinion on a horse. Tell me, what do you know about that *Eternal Hope* colt." "Leave him alone. Leave him alone, Mr. Pendleton. Don't touch him." "Jim," I said, "I'm not going to buy him. All I want is his story." "Well," said Jim, "I don't know all the story but maybe most of it. Old man Wilkins bred him in Kentucky, and he was one of the best looking yearlings I ever saw sold at Saratoga. I tried to get my people to buy him because I figured he was bred on his dam's side to go an extra quarter, but they said times were bad, and I had to stop at $10,000 and he sold for $16,000. I don't know but what I was mighty lucky, but then again maybe I wasn't. He was one of those burnt-out yearlings that had been stuffed for the sales. Well, the people who bought him wanted to get him to the track as fast as they could and race him down South. You never saw a colt go to pieces so quick, and he has been going from bad to worse ever since. He got to feeding poor, and they give him enough rubbish to poison an elephant. You know, Mr. Pendleton, no colt that don't feel good is going to run, and there ain't a mite of good in taking a bat to him. You got to get him feeling good first, and then if he won't run, get rid of him. This colt ain't felt good since he started to train and he hates racing and won't try. He has a burst of speed but won't run far enough to get warm in August. If you touch him with a bat he's like as not to back up with you. He's changed hands three or four times. He's done as a race horse all right, but some of you hunting people might use him if you could get a pound of flesh on him. There is one thing I like about him mighty well and that's his action. He's about the sweetest moving horse I've seen since *Colin's* day. Some old codger bought him at the sale. He didn't have anything to lead him away with, and I told one of my boys to let him have a halter shank and he thanked me as though I had given him a service to *Man o' War*." I thanked Andrews and went off to see the next race.

June slipped into July, and I went off on my annual cruise. On my return I was exceedingly busy and seldom went into the village, with the result that I saw nothing of the Major. We passed each other on the road now and again but never visited together.

About the second week in September I had occasion to go into our back country. Years before I had taken over a tract of land near Woolville. The property lay in two townships and I was having an altercation with the Woolville Assessors.

Twenty-five years ago Woolville had been quite a trotting horse center but through the closing of the mills the countryside was slowly disintegrating. I had not been there for many years.

It was eighteen miles over an atrocious road to the Village Hall where the Assessors were sitting and had made an appointment for me to meet with them.

When about a half mile from the town I saw the old trotting track down in the valley to my right. It was a dreary sight. The grandstand, stabling and rail had pretty much gone to pieces, and I was thinking upon the ups and downs of such institutions and those who stick to them too long when to my surprise I saw something moving on the weed covered track. I stopped the car and presently it became clear that some one was riding a horse. I would have been a good deal surprised to have seen a trotter being jogged to a sulky but to see any one riding a horse in Woolville was a phenomenon.

Ahead of me was a lane which apparently ran down to the track. I turned the car into the lane, and when half way down I saw that there was an automobile parked near the track, and a person, probably the owner of the car, was standing at the rail.

Just as I reached the track the horse and rider walked past me, and there, to my utter surprise was Ephraim Jackson sitting as big as life on a very fit-looking thoroughbred colt. The look of horror which spread over Ephraim's face when he recognized me, conveyed a message, and I would gladly have retired from the scene, but he was certain to tell his employer that he had seen me, so it seemed far better to go over and speak with the Major, which I did. If he regretted my intrusion he certainly gave no sign of it and for my part I thoroughly enjoyed watching the Major work his colt, cool him out and put him away. Every morning for three months the old gentleman had been up at the crack of dawn and humped eighteen miles over the worst stretch of road in our county to devote the knowledge and experience of his seventy-seven years to the rejuvenation and training of his colt.

Starting with a sour, poisoned, unhappy young horse he had produced one with a sheen to his coat, a keen sparkle in his eye and an urge to run. His account of the accomplishment of this was a monograph on the care of the thoroughbred horse. The description of his trials in teaching Ephraim to ride touched every chord from deep pathos to hilarity.

When the work on the track was finished we took to our cars and followed the colt down the road to Silas Hemphill's farm. Hemphill was an old trotting-horse man from whom the Major had begged a stall and whom he had persuaded to feed and keep an eye on the colt. In speaking of Hemphill the Major said, "Mr. Hemphill has given me much valuable assistance. It is regrettable, Suh, to see so much knowledge wasted upon these trotting-bred horses."

The task of putting *Eternal Hope* away was a ceremony of some pretensions. When the finishing touches had been put on and we were about to close his box the Major said, "Mr. Pendleton, Suh, it has been a great pleasure, I might say a very great pleasure to have you see my colt work, but might I presume upon you, Suh, to make no mention of the affair to any of our friends? My horse is not quite ready. I'm sure you will understand, Suh."

I continued on to my appointment with the Assessors who, thinking that I had forgotten the engagement, had adjourned, boding ill for me in so far as my Woolville assessments went.

Some two weeks later I was attending a meeting of the Board of Governors of the Hunt Club and listening to Jimmie

Atkinson, the Treasurer, reading his report in a singsong voice when Colonel Weatherford who was sitting next to me reached in his pocket and handed me a special delivery letter addressed to him, saying, "Read that. I have just received it from Jim Parkins." It was a letter from the Major.

James H. Parkins and John Weatherford, Esquires,
Trustees of the Dulaney Denning Trust Estate,
New York City.
Gentlemen:

I write you about a matter of the very highest importance. This is to inform you that two weeks from today I am starting my colt, *Eternal Hope*, in the famous and historic Great American Stakes of a guaranteed value of $40,000. The fact that no member of my family has ever won this important event has been a great incentive to me during moments of passing discouragement, and the fine attitude which my colt has maintained towards the meagre facilities at my command gives assurance of his generosity and heart.

I was somewhat surprised in examining into my affairs this afternoon to discover that my bank account was neither what I thought it to be, nor would wish it to be in view of the many important arrangements yet to be made before my horse can go to the post. In fact, gentlemen, my friend, Mr. Whitlock, the Cashier of my Bank, with whom I have conferred, informs me that my balance is eight dollars and nine cents. In response to Mr. Whitlock's inquiry as to whether there might be further checks outstanding, a matter on which he seemed to place some import, I was obliged to explain to him that of course a person could not be sure of such things.

I have made a most careful calculation of my needs in connection with the starting of my colt and will ask you to sell sufficient of the securities in my trust estate to permit of your remitting me one thousand dollars.

I am quite aware that this will deplete the estate but only temporarily for I shall shortly restore the amount. This is a small matter, gentlemen, when compared with having the name of Denning enrolled among the names of the other famous racing families who have won this historic stake.

Of the sum I have asked for I have included $500 which I purpose wagering on my colt. For my own honor, and as a tribute to the fine spirit and generosity of my horse, I can hazard no less an amount.

As time presses I shall hope to hear from you by return of post. I remain, gentlemen,

Yours to command,

DULANEY DENNING.

I returned the letter to the envelope, handed it back to the Colonel, and tried to pay some decent attention to Jimmie Atkinson's report but in my then frame of mind I was but little concerned that the Hunt had purchased a new hunt horse for $600, or that we had paid $30 damages resulting from some one leaving a barway down, thereby giving Mr. Sweetser's cows the freedom of Mrs. Thompson's corn.

My mind was entirely taken up with the picture of a small colored boy galloping a chestnut colt among the weeds of the deserted Woolville trotting track and a solitary old man leaning over the broken-down rail watching him, and the colt being put away in a makeshift boxstall attached to the end of Silas Hemphill's cattle barn. Then another picture came to me. I saw the great race track with fifty thousand people present to watch the best colts of the year, some said of the decade, race for one of the most coveted of all stakes. "A small matter, gentlemen, compared with having the name of Denning enrolled among the names of the other famous racing families who have won this historic stake." The pathos of it all struck me and I wanted to get away from the meeting with its inconsequential prattle. Then I was conscious of hearing Mr. Dennison, the President, say, "If there is nothing more to bring up, gentlemen, the Chair will entertain a motion to adjourn."

As I shoved my chair back Colonel Weatherford said, "Pendleton, if you are not engaged will you dine with me tonight?" I said I would.

We had a delightful dinner together. As the Colonel was raising his first spoonful of soup to his mouth he put it down again and said to the butler, "Have you uncorked the wine?" "Not yet, Sir." Then turning to me he said, "That letter seems to have upset me. I feel like a particularly good bottle of wine," and he instructed his man to bring a bottle of especially fine Chambertin.

No further reference was made to the Major but as we were having coffee and a pony of his 1839 brandy in the library, he went over to his desk, found the letter, and stretching out his long legs towards the fire, re-read it to himself in a slow, deliberate way and sat staring into the fire. Then he said more to himself than to me:

"The Great American Stakes. Why there hasn't been a year in the last quarter of a century when that Stake will be as hard to win as this very year. I can't imagine any trainer sending a horse to the post to chase *Whisk Boy* and *Ultimatum* for a mile and a half. A struggle like that is very apt to break a generous colt's heart and keep him out of training for a season. Where is this colt of Denning's? Is it the thing he bought at the auction at Belmont Park last spring? Why I had forgotten all about the matter. Who is training for him? Now he wants $1000 and $500 of it is to wager that he will beat the two best colts in the United States. God bless my soul! Pendleton, did you ever hear of such a business?"

In view of the Major's letter telling of his plans I could see no harm in recounting my chance visit to the Woolville track. When I had finished the Colonel got up, found his pipe, lit it, and took a turn or two of the room. At last he said, "We must not forget that the old man is a past master at some things. If he wasn't heading his colt for that particular stake I might take some interest in the matter, but the thing is preposterous. It's idiotic, and worse than that it's wasteful," and he went on smoking his pipe and thinking. Then he asked me if I knew what time the Major worked the colt in the morning and I told him at eight o'clock, and that it was an hour and a half's drive to the track as the road was worse than an abandoned corduroy road in the State of Maine.

He walked over to the side of the room and rang a bell. When the butler appeared he ordered breakfast for a quarter before six and asked him to send Albert to him. He told Albert he wished him to make sure from the chauffeur that the Ford station wagon was in running order, to have the jack and all tools in the car together with two spares, and that he wanted him, not the chauffeur, to accompany him at 6:30 in the morning. He asked me what I was doing in the morning, and I told him I had to go to New York.

My mind kept reverting to the Major's urgent plea for

the $1000 and I didn't want to go home that night without knowing what his chances were of getting it so I finally asked point blank whether the trustees would sell the securities and let the Major have the money.

At first the Colonel seemed reluctant to discuss the matter and disposed to pass it off. Then of a sudden he sat down, turned his chair until he faced me and said, "Pendleton, there is no trust estate. There never was. There are no securities. I am the trust estate. Dulaney Denning and I have been friends for nearly fifty years. We owned a good race horse together forty-eight years ago when I was only a youngster. Jim Parkins and I went down to the Kentucky Derby a few years ago and found the old man absolutely destitute. He can no more resist gambling than I can subsist without food. His friends had long since despaired of aiding him. Jim Parkins invented and worked out this trust estate idea. Jim discovered that the old man had a thousand shares of stock of a defunct oil company that had been out of business for ten years. Denning knew nothing about the stock except that the young sharper who had sold it to him told him to hold on to it. I was to buy the stock but only on the condition that the funds were to be turned over to Jim and placed in a trust fund and Denning was to receive a fixed income.

"Jim sends him money from time to time and charges it to my account. I was afraid to leave the old man in the environs of Kentucky, so insisted as part of the arrangement that he come here to live, where I could keep an eye on him for he is getting along. I fixed up the room at Mrs. Martin's for him. To follow the races in the newspapers, and make a bet now and again is meat and drink to him. He couldn't live without it, so we send him a few dollars each month for this purpose. I have tried to make him decently comfortable but it is futile to do more than this because if I did he would become involved. Last spring he hit the thing right four or five times in succession and pyramided and ended up with $2800, with which he bought the colt and his car and the Great American Stakes is the result."

Having learned the status of the trust estate I could hardly refer again to the Major's suggestion that securities be sold and as we were both scheduled to rise early I left the Colonel and walked home across my lower meadow in the moonlight thinking about this matter.

In the morning I purchased every paper known to contain even a vestige of sporting news and read all the news referring to the Great American Stakes. The Colonel had diagnosed the situation correctly. Some sport writers thought there might be four starters. One prophesied a field of five, but the better-informed doubted whether any third horse would contest with *Whisk Boy* and *Ultimatum*.

The business which took me to New York seemed to drag on interminably, and it was a Thursday before I finally reached home and the great race was to be run on Saturday. I had tried to reach Colonel Weatherford once or twice but with no success, and, of course, had heard nothing about the Major or his colt.

Immediately upon reaching home I called the Colonel's house but Albert told me the Colonel had left that morning for Long Island where he had gone to visit and would return Sunday or Monday, and told me with whom he was staying. I then hurried down to the village in quest of the Major. Mrs. Martin met me with the information that the Major and Ephraim had started for Long Island in the car and would be back Sunday or Monday. According to Mrs. Martin the car was messed up with what she referred to as horse trappings. It was quite evident that poor Mrs. Martin had a very great deal preying on her mind that morning, and was in sore need of a confidant. I would willingly have stayed to talk with her but was hesitant just then about entering into any discussion of the Major's affairs.

When I arrived at Mrs. Martin's I had seen Mrs. Hattie Jackson, Ephraim's mother, sitting on the end of Mrs. Martin's porch. Mrs. Jackson was without any doubt the most portly woman in our village, and in spite of the fact that it was a brisk mid-September day and I had a light overcoat on, Mrs. Jackson was sitting on Mrs. Martin's porch fanning herself with a newspaper. She was certainly exercised about something.

Mrs. Martin's porch stands eighteen or twenty feet back from the sidewalk and there is a rickety gate separating Mrs. Martin's property from the outside world. In leaving I was delayed through trying to make the gate swing away from me when its designer had planned otherwise, and in this interval I heard Mrs. Jackson say to Mrs. Martin:

"Mrs. Martin, mam, las' night I done talk to de Lord fo' most fifteen minutes and I say over and over — Lord — make him run fas' fo' old Major's sake. Make him run fas' — and Lord, you keep a smart lookout on my Ephraim, mussed up with all them reptiles and sinners at that ole race track;" and I heard Mrs. Martin say, "Hattie, I don't know very much about all these things, only I'm worried about what will happen to the old Major if his horse doesn't do what he expects him to do. The night before last he sent Ephraim to ask if he could speak with me and when I went

to him he had two glasses of grape juice and he said, 'Mam'
— in that way he has of saying it — 'Mam, would you do
me the honor of toasting the success of my horse?' Now I
haven't been brought up in those sort of ways. I don't know
whatever my old mother would have thought of it, but I held
my glass up like he did, and we both drank the grape juice,
and his face and eyes were that excited like. I don't understand much about what's going on, but the day after Mr.
Whitlock was here, the Major took away those two silver
mugs and his tray what he set such store in and was away all
day and I haven't seen them since."

On my way home from the village I discovered that during
my short absence the Colonel's horse van had returned from
a trip, for it was in the ditch a quarter of a mile from the
Colonel's entrance. In endeavoring to pass a delivery wagon
which came dashing out of Enid Ashley's driveway, Eddie
Walsh had let the van slip off the road. Eddie, who always
drove the van, was in no pleasant mood and blurted out that
it was all on account of the Colonel lending his van to every
Tom, Dick and Harry, and wasn't he this very minute but
coming home from Long Island from taking some sort of a
selling plater belonging to that Major Denning who lived at
Mrs. Martin's, to the track. Not being able to follow Eddie's
logic I left him after promising to 'phone to the Colonel's
for aid. I had at least learned that the colt had arrived safely
at the track.

When I reached home I found a long telegram from the
Colonel waiting for me. It read:

"Hope you can meet me Steward's Room at track twelve
Saturday stop Please go Silas Hemphill's and get gray cat

that slept in stall with Denning's colt stop Secure it safely and send cat by Eddie Walsh in car to track and deliver to Major in person stop I want Walsh to start immediately regardless of the hour and wait at McPherson's Stable until the Major arrives stop Wire Jim Andrews phone me Westbury 896.

JOHN WEATHERFORD."

I attended to the matters covered in the telegram and thoroughly enjoyed the expression on Eddie Walsh's face as I read him the instructions in the telegram and handed him the gray cat which was to serve as a companion and sedative for the "selling plater."

I was on the road too early Saturday morning to procure any newspaper but stopped at the first town where I thought they would be available and sat on the bench of a dreary railroad station of an equally dreary town and turned to the sporting page. "A three horse field promised for the Great American Stakes. All the good horses in training decline to contend the issue with *Whisk Boy* and *Ultimatum*. An outsider to gallop the course in the wake of the stars. D. Denning's well-named *Eternal Hope* the only other contender." Then followed a eulogistic account of the prowess of the two colts and their previous achievements. There was a short paragraph at the end to the effect that the Denning colt had proved himself a high-priced washout. I climbed back in my car and proceeded to break a great many local speed ordinances.

I met the Colonel at twelve o'clock and we went in search of a table which he had reserved for luncheon. "Pendleton," he said, "without one single exception this is the most miserable situation into which I have ever been injected. It's not the financial aspect of it. That's nothing. It's the element of tragedy that churns up one's feelings and emotions. I have done everything I can think of to dissuade the old man from starting his colt. I have had Jim Andrews talk to him and we have both begged him to wait and slip the colt into some easy seven-furlong event. This Andrews of yours is a royal fellow. He has even promised to take the colt into his own string for a month free of expense. I went as far as badgering poor Jim Parkins to come over here last night from Greenwich. Denning considers him the personification of all wisdom and Jim talked to him for two hours, but to no avail. Andrews is persuaded the colt is yellow. Even the Major admits you daren't touch him with a bat.

"Pendleton, it's difficult to forecast what the effect is going to be on Denning of having his colt trail along for a mile and then completely close up. Those two colts are going to burn that track up this afternoon. Mark my words, that *Ultimatum* colt is going to run the mile faster than any horse in this country ever ran a mile over the mile and a half route. It takes a horse of super-courage — super-courage, Pendleton, to keep on trying in the face of a thing like that. I still believe the *Whisk Boy* colt will catch him and beat him in the last quarter, but I'll wager that neither *Whisk Boy* or his owner will ever forget this race.

"All Denning will say is that his colt has always done what he has asked him to do and done it with high courage. God bless me, Pendleton, what can you tell about high courage by working a colt around a bumpy weed-covered tract with a boy up who can't decently jog a horse let alone breeze him. I don't see why the colt hasn't broken his four legs and the boy's neck long before this.

[37]

"When you get to my age friendship and affections and long associations count for a great deal and I would have done anything in my power to have preserved my old friend from disappointment, but the die has been cast. I had Parkins give him the $1000 he wanted. As a matter of fact I felt so badly when I saw him all alone over at that dreary Woolville track standing knee deep in the weeds and watching his colt, and thought of all the mornings he had been doing that same thing that I asked Jim to send him an extra $500. Jim wrote him that it was an accumulation of surplus. He has $1000 on his colt. The astounding odds are proof enough of the money having been thrown away but I don't really care. A few dollars is of little moment when compared with some other things."

I am not apt to forget that afternoon's racing, for I have a score of pictures that linger on in my memory.

I was set upon seeing the horses saddled and, knowing that there would be an unprecedented crowd at the paddock because of the publicity being given to this famous horse duel, I took my place early at the paddock rail. Every racing enthusiast on the grounds wanted to compare one colt with the other for they had never met before.

Whisk Boy was the first to arrive. He was a large, impressive colt of great scope — really a super-thoroughbred. A minute later *Ultimatum* was led in. He was a horse of very different type — a smaller, tight knit horse that had run everything he had yet met completely off their feet up to a mile and a quarter. Nothing was to be seen of *Eternal Hope.*

In the meantime Colonel Weatherford had squeezed in beside me. As we stood there he said, "The old man is so afraid of awakening bad memories in his colt that he will not bring him out until the last second." Then Ephraim appeared leading the colt followed by the Major and Jim Andrews.

Jim put the saddle on while the Major stood at his colt's head and held him.

There was no doubt about there being a lot of very surprised horsemen around that paddock when the colt was uncovered. I had to smile to see Joe Lefferts who, they say, has made a couple of million dollars at the tracks, open his mouth and turn and fairly run towards the grandstand.

How few of us ever experience a sense of high exultation, yet I think old Major Denning standing there with his colt came as near to it as most of us will ever come. The love of a big-hearted, lonely old man alienated from kith, kin and home, was concentrated on that horse and the thought came to me that on that colt's efforts during the next few minutes — on his will to run — his will to give generously of his all — would depend the whole course of the old man's few remaining years. The other two colts were owned by men of fabulous wealth to whom to win meant only one more victory.

The bugle sounded and the jockeys were put up. The Major had procured a comparatively unknown boy to ride his colt. It was all he could get. The parade and journey to the post were soon over, for the start at the mile and a half distance is in front of the stands. *Ultimatum* tried the patience of the starter for a few minutes, and then I heard the Colonel's stop-watch click and they were off to a perfect start. Figuratively speaking I squared my shoulders to take what came and make the best of it, and wished I had not been caught standing between the Major and Colonel Weatherford when the flag dropped.

Ultimatum, with the sizzling speed for which he was famous, jumped into the lead and opened up daylight between himself and *Whisk Boy* while *Eternal Hope* trailed three lengths behind. They ran thus to the half-mile post, and out of the corner of my eye I saw the Colonel look at his watch and heard him utter a soft grunt. Then *Whisk Boy* made a bid and closed the gap, and held on for an eighth and dropped back. It took no watch to tell me that the pace was terrific. At the mile I saw the Colonel again look at his watch and heard him mutter, "God bless me." As they were passing the mile post *Whisk Boy* made the second of his three famous challenges which endeared him to all race lovers who saw that race, again closed the gap and held on for perhaps an eighth — and again was shaken off. There were fifty thousand people prepared to acclaim *Ultimatum* the speed marvel of the age. *Eternal Hope* was trailing five lengths in the rear but running smoothly and the boy was sitting like a statue. Jim Andrews was right when he said he was a beautiful mover.

They were just approaching the mile and a quarter when *Whisk Boy* came on again and for the third time was on even terms with his rival and this time could not be shaken off; I heard the Major say, "The gamest horse, Suh, I ever saw run." The horses were rounding the turn and coming into the stretch with *Whisk Boy's* head a shade in front. Fifty thousand people around me were shouting for their favorites as I have never heard a racing crowd shout before or since. Then of a sudden the shouting subsided. The chestnut colt was closing up the gap and the three horses were thundering down the track to the finish.

The boys on the two leaders went to their bats. Then I saw *Ultimatum* commence to drop back and the chestnut colt caught him and passed him. The shouts of the crowd had fallen to a murmur. I saw the Colonel cast an anxious glance at Denning, and hastily put his brawny arm within the Major's. The unbeaten *Whisk Boy* was still running magnificently, and with that tremendous stride which all turf writers had described as a killing thing, yet the chestnut colt had reached his girths and was holding on.

It seemed certain that the race must end that way when of a sudden the Major's boy lifted his bat and gave it a quick flourish but did not touch the colt. It had been as plain as day to the Major's jockey that if he did not do something *Whisk Boy* must win. He, therefore, shook his bat. These horses had run that particular course faster than it had ever been run before but in spite of that the chestnut colt made a flash-like response. There was no man or woman in that great seething, swaying crowd that could have questioned his gameness. The Major had said he had high courage and he had. I have seen men strain to win foot races at every distance from a hundred yards up and seen them give their last ounce. I took my place in a shell for four years and in so far as I could judge myself, I gave my last ounce or tried to. I have stood spellbound at Cambridge, Princeton and New Haven and seen men break away with the football with no one between them and the goal while eighty thousand people cheered and waved or held their breath and watched the last ounce being given by him who ran and them who pursued. I think I know when the last ounce is being given. As a matter of fact the whole world — every man, woman and child — knows and becomes electrified.

If I ever saw a horse giving his last ounce, if I ever saw the very last fraction of an ounce being given, it was when I watched Dulaney Denning's *Eternal Hope* trying to catch and beat *Whisk Boy*. He had never been touched by heel or whip. He just strained and struggled on out of sheer gameness and out of the will to run. He struggled inch by inch until he was at *Whisk Boy's* throat latch. There he seemed to stop and he dwelt there a second. They had but a few lengths to go. Then once again I saw the chestnut's head slowly creeping up. Then they were even. For a stride the horses' heads were together, then it was over. *Eternal Hope* by *Eternal,* the property of Major Dulaney Denning of Kentucky had won the forty-ninth renewal of the Great American Stakes.

When I turned to the Major he had removed his hat — I remember removing mine, and saw the Colonel do the same, and I held out my hand. He straightened himself up and made an effort to say something, but only made me a deep bow and then turned and shook hands with the Colonel.

We helped him down to the track where Jim Andrews was waiting with a halter shank — a leather one with a polished brass snap on it. "Here, Major," he said, "I've been holding this in my hand all during the race hoping you were going to need it. Lead him in with it. It's a better one than I lent you the day you bought him."

Even after all these years a film of mist is prone to cross my eyes when I recall the picture of the old Major at that moment. I had always thought of him as ageless and robust, but as I looked at him exercising the prerogative of that particular race, that an owner shall lead in his winning horse, he looked frail and drawn, and I had an impulse to shield and help him. He was surrounded by a sea of eager, pressing faces. Behind the Major, dazed and bewildered and not grasping or comprehending one-half of what was happening, walked Ephraim Washington Jackson.

We accompanied the Major while he received the gold vase which always goes with the stake. We all knew that the result of the race had been a bitter sentimental disappointment to the President of the Association, but he certainly permitted no tinge of it to appear; as he handed the vase to the Major he said, "Major Denning it is indeed a genuine pleasure for us to see this trophy won by a gentleman from Kentucky, and we congratulate you, Sir, on being the owner of so royally bred and stout-hearted a colt. We wish you further successes with him on the track and hope that he may breed on in the stud."

The Major accepted the vase and said, "Mr. President, Suh, this trophy will remain in the archives of the Dennings as one of their most cherished possessions. It was my highest ambition, Suh, to have the name of Denning enrolled among the other illustrious racing families who have won this great stake. I thank you, Suh." And the ceremony was over.

As soon as we could arrange it we carried the Major off to a quiet table and persuaded him to sit down, and we three old friends sat down together. Such comments and remarks as occur to one at such moments strike one as being inconsequential and flat, so we said nothing for a minute or two, then the Major turned to me and said, "Would you render me a service, Suh? Would you dispatch a message to my good landlady, Mrs. Martin, and say this to her. Say I have been successful in the affair I had in hand and am coming home. And one more thing Mr. Pendleton, if you would be so kind, would you dispatch a message to Mr. Parkins and say that my trust estate has been restored. Thank you, Suh."

CHAPTER IV.

Cub Hunting en Famille

SEEING the Colonel's horse van going out of his driveway, I asked him whether he was acquiring a new horse or shipping one away. "It's going over to Pettibone Lithgow's," he said. Pettibone is one of the best hearted people alive and we are deservedly fond of him but he does not possess a vestige of horse sense.

"Pendleton, have you ever stopped to consider what a mass of detailed information one acquires pertaining to horses? Why even were I able to extract it I couldn't reduce within the covers of ten volumes the sum total of what any one of a thousand knowledgeable horsemen knows. Such information is only released from the confines of one's memory when a situation develops requiring its use. And no man knows more than an infinitesimal part of what is to be learned.

"Yet here is our friend Pettibone good naturedly smiling and romping along, endangering his family and his friends and not knowing what it's all about. It is common knowledge that he is going to hurt, kill or maim one or both of these children of his if he continues in over-mounting them on over-fed, over-bred, under-worked and under-schooled horses.

"Mrs. Lithgow came over to see me about it. She says they haven't a horse on the place fit for the children to ride, al-

[45]

though Pettibone has spent a pot of money trying to mount them. She is fairly distraught about that play-boy husband of hers.

"I have loaned them *Lord Autumn* for one of the children. I think the old fellow will enjoy the job.

"What a time Pettibone must have had two weeks ago on the morning we started cubbing. Enid Ashley has pieced her interpretation of the events together. Wait until I read her account to you."

CUB HUNTING EN FAMILLE

CHAPTER I.

An opulent office at 14 Wall Street, New York. A conference of people of importance. It is four o'clock on a Friday afternoon in early September.

J. Pettibone Lithgow: "Gentlemen, I must ask you to excuse me. I must run for my train. Tomorrow is the opening of our cubbing season. It is an event I look forward to with keen relish. We are taking our children for their first hunt, and we all place great import on the occasion. It is indeed many years since I have looked forward to anything with such genuine relish. I return to town on Monday morning, and will meet with you any time during the week. Good day, gentlemen."

CHAPTER II.

A so-called simple hunting lodge with eleven bathrooms, and service and embellishments to match. Dinner is being served.

J. Pettibone Lithgow: "Well, children, tomorrow will be

the big day. I feel just as I did when I was your age and it was the night before Christmas. Now, then, what are we all going to ride? First, there is Mother. What about *Big Brother?*"

Chorus: "Yes, yes. He's an old dear. He's top hole."

Pettibone Lithgow: "Well, how about it, Mother?"

Mrs. J. Pettibone Lithgow: "I love to ride the old fellow, but do so dislike bustling him up and down these rocky wood rides in the cubbing country. They are abominable coverts."

Pettibone Lithgow: "That's all right. We won't go hard. Remember this is the children's first day to hounds. What for Lillian? Withington says that *Lady Conna* and *Shinto* are going perfectly, and Lillian has been riding both of them. Which one will it be, old girl?"

Lillian Lithgow (aged 12): "Oh, Dad, I want *Shinto*. He is so cute over his fences."

Pettibone Lithgow: "Then that leaves Pettibone and the Old Man. My boy, what do you think will carry you to fame and honor tomorrow?"

Pettibone Lithgow, Jr. (aged 14): "I would like very much to try *Aunt Agnes*. I have been jumping her a lot and we get on fine."

Pettibone Lithgow: "Well, I will ride *Hecanhopit*. This will be our tenth season together." (To Butler) "Ask Withington to see me in the library in half an hour. It's time you kiddies turned in. All hands up at 4:45. No stealing of cat naps, remember." (Children leave the room. To Wife) "My dear, this is an event I have been looking forward to ever since the children were born. My day dreams have centered on pictures of us all spending long days together in the hunting field. Countless times I have pictured you and the two

[47]

kiddies mounted on truly confidential horses drifting across an autumn landscape. You know, dear, I have worked pretty hard in a highly competitive field, and this thing tomorrow morning is one of my major rewards."

CHAPTER III.

4:55 a.m.

Pettibone, Jr.: "Mother, I can't find my jodphurs, and Mary is not awake so I can't ask her, and Lillie says one of her riding shoes is gone, and she says she remembers the puppy was playing with it, and do you think he could have run off with it?"

Mrs. Lithgow: "It's too bad you children could not have found your things before you went to bed. I will be there in a minute."

Mr. Lithgow: "My dear, I wonder where those special hunting spectacles could be. I haven't seen them since last fall. It is getting late. We must hurry."

Pettibone, Jr.: "Moth - er (louder) Moth - er — (louder still) MOTH - ER — Where is the hunting crop Uncle Harry gave me for Christmas?"

Mr. Pettibone Lithgow (calling from the dining room): "We must hurry. Breakfast is on the table."

Mrs. Lithgow: "John, I can't hurry. The children can't find half their things, and I'm not nearly ready. Such an hour to get children up."

(Mr. L. drinks his coffee and fidgets. Family assembles in the breakfast room, Mrs. L. looking a bit frayed and distraught.)

Mr. L.: "I will hack to the Meet with the children, and

Mother, you come in the car. Come along, children."

(They go out to the stable, mount and start. An exceedingly warm sultry morning. *Shinto*, feeling high, makes a modest buck.)

Mr. L.: "There now Lillie, there goes your hat the first thing. Don't dismount. That horse is so high — you will have trouble remounting. Pettibone, pop off and get your sister's hat. That's a good chap. I'll hold *Aunt Agnes*." (Holds horse which dribbles and slobbers half-consumed sugar on the knee of a new pair of fawn breeches. They walk up on the side of a cement road. At the corner they meet other riders. Lillie permits *Shinto* to walk up on the heels of a fidgety mare who lets fly, just missing Lillie's leg.)

Mr. L.: "Lillie for gracious sake keep your horse back. You should know better than that. Pray excuse my daughter, Mrs. Turnturtle. She has been told not to ride on top of people. Pettibone, will you keep off that slippery cement! How many times have you been told to keep on the side of the road. Press your *Aunt Agnes* on the ribs with your left heel and bring her over."

(A particularly noisy truck approaches from the rear. Horses in front commence to fidget. Truck passes with a roar. *Aunt Agnes* makes a moderate fly jump to the right. Steps in hidden ditch and pecks. J. Pettibone Lithgow, Jr. topples over her shoulder and lets go of reins. A groom catches mare, puts boy up and receives a dollar. Pettibone's face and collar are smeared. Mr. Lithgow is hot and becoming twitchy. Arrive at Meet. Renews many old acquaintanceships. Introduces children. Rather proud of them, but wishes boy did not look so mussy. Spirits temporarily revived. Mrs. L. arrives. Finds her horse for her. Puts her up. No coordination. Starts to count three. She does not wait for count. Never will for some reason. Comes near throwing her clean over the side saddle. Mob of people looking on. Mrs. L. a bit peeved. Busies himself adjusting balance strap. Hounds move off. Wishes all members of the family would stay together. There is Lillie away up in front, riding with loose reins and letting her horse crowd upon everybody. May get kicked. Would like to call out to her, but hates to bellow like that.)

Mrs. L.: "I'm sorry, John, but the saddle is resting right on *Big Brother's* withers. I really should have a sheepskin."

Mr. L.: "Well, *Shinto* is the only horse out with a sheepskin. I will get it for you." (Weaves way up front. Locates Lillie and pulls to side of road. When the field has passed, he takes sheepskin from *Shinto* and puts it on *Big Brother.* Gets very warm and feels mussy.

(Family jiggle jaggles down the road. *Aunt Agnes* determined to catch up with field, commences to yaw, and it is evident boy cannot hold her. Gets horse stopped, dismounts and starts to tighten curb. Mare makes quick turn of head and breaks brim of new hunting derby. Mounts and they proceed. Foot prints show that field has entered a meadow. Wishes they might have been with the field so that some one else might have slipped the rails. Dismounts and slips three obdurate chestnut rails. *Shinto* in exuberance jumps three feet over the bars and bucks on landing. Lillie loses hat and one stirrup but stays on. Picks up hat and tries to hand it to daughter, but horse will not let him approach. With mounting irritation crams hat in pocket and goes back to build up bar way. Mounts and they start across meadow. Feels in pocket for gloves. Can only find one, new pair, hates riding without gloves. Goes back to bar way but can't find other glove. Begins to feel all on edge. Sees the field at end of meadow against fringe of woods. Hears hounds open and sees field disappear up wood ride. Suggest they all jog. Try to jog but horses very keen and start cantering and continually going faster in spite of his protests and volley of instructions. They start up wood road, turn corner, and come upon whole field galloping towards them. A moment of awful suspense — Exhorts family to do this and that. Pulls *Hecanhopit* up so short that Mrs. L. plows into him. Bellows to Lillie to stop her horse which she does with horse standing clear across the ride. Huntsman forces his way between *Shinto's* quarters and oak tree by lifting both legs high in air. Entire field stewing, mulling, steaming, and trying to get by and on. L. gets excited and says, "Pettibone, I wish you would kick your *Aunt Agnes* in the ribs, and make her move over," upon which a passing wag mutters something which irritates yet emphasizes the inappropriateness of the horse's name. The field passes on. Family reorganizes and follows on. Upon reaching meadow they turn right-handed and start up another ride. Set of bars just ahead. Mrs. L. charges. *Big Brother* refuses. Mrs. L. within an ace of flopping off on near side. The affair gives him quite a turn. Pettibone, Jr. pleads to give Mother a lead. Charges. Mare stands away and makes an unexpectedly big jump. Pettibone, Jr. lands on rear of saddle, losing left stirrup and reins, and so disappears around turn. What in the world will happen to the boy? He tells wife and daughter to wait. Sends *Hecanhopit* along at fence. Overtakes boy who is quite intact. Boy tries to explain. L. very short with his heir. Returns to barway. Mrs. L. and daughter navigate jump very creditably. All hands hasten up the ride. Can hear hounds away up towards top of ridge. They keep plugging along, turning now right, now left, through a maze of paths. They can detect no footprints. Which way *has* field gone? Mounting a slight swale they hear hounds coming right at them. Stop their horses. Know only too well that Huntsman, M.F.H., and field will be along directly, and they will be accused of heinous crimes. Hounds come on with a gorgeous burst of voice, and come right up to where they are all huddled. Their horses must be standing on and soiling the very line of the hunted fox. Mr. Pettibone Lithgow would give half he possessed to be any place else in the world. Hounds' heads go up. There is not a whimper to be heard. If only one hound would go over them, under them, around them, and find the line and go on. Would he dare exhort them and try and cast them? Takes a chance — removes new hat with broken rim — waves hounds on — Hoick — Hoick — Hoick — Hoick forrard, indicating the supposed line. His voice sounds odd and unfamiliar. Hears horses galloping back of him. Looks. Huntsman appears, closely followed by M.F.H. and entire field. The family completely surrounded by hounds. Mr. L. starts to move away.)

M.F.H.: "Hold hard, sir, Hold hard. You have either turned this fox, or at least have all heads in the air. Let the hounds hunt the fox. That's what they are for. You can't catch him with your hands."

(Whole family upset. Children take it very seriously. Mr. L. believes the worst is over — when the wood resounds with pitiful lamentations. *Aunt Agnes* has kicked a hound.)

The M.F.H.: "What horse has kicked that hound?"

Mr. L.: "It was my son's mare. She is an experienced hunter and never did such a thing before."

(M.F.H. says nothing and rides on. A hound feathers a

[52]

short way down the slope — opens — is honored by the pack, and the field moves on.)

Mrs. L.: "John, I really have quite a headache. If you don't mind I think I will pull out."

Mr. L.: "Well, my dear, I think we have had enough for our first day out."

CHAPTER V.

Enid Ashley's Knight Errant

THERE is no denying the fact that our community was in a blue funk. We were on the verge of losing Enid Ashley and the event was painful and distressing beyond words. It's a long story but the pertinent facts are that George Ashley had been caught in "the Market;" then whatever caught him squeezed him, and finally completely annihilated him financially. With his powers of resistance at a low ebb, he had journeyed up to Cambridge for the Yale game, shivered through two hours, and that which "the Market" started, double pneumonia finished.

When the young man in Wedgewood, Stacey & Murdock's law office, in whose particular province George's estate lay, had sifted this and delved into that, he finally brought his file into Tom Murdock's sanctum. Tom Murdock had been a great crony of George's. They were forever going off fishing or shooting together, and at one time had owned jointly a couple of race horses.

At the end of fifteen minutes Tom's face wore a very grave look. He was a great admirer of Enid Ashley, as we all were, and his mind reverted to three small kiddies out in a lovely old stone farmhouse in the country, and to a lot of other things in which he found little comfort.

He again consulted a long sheet of paper containing a great

many items which the young man had labeled Schedule A, and another sheet marked Schedule B, with very few items listed thereon, turned his swivel chair around and looked out over New York Bay. He sat thus for some minutes, asked the young man if he was quite sure there was nothing else, and then the young man and the file left the office. As he was going out of the door Murdock said, "When you get ready to prepare a bill in this Estate please see me about it personally." I never saw the two sheets of paper that caused Tom to look out over New York Bay, but we all knew without being told that there was next to nothing left.

At such moments and in such situations people surprise you and surprise themselves by the genuineness of their desire to help. We did try to help, but nothing ever seemed to materialize. Enid tried real estate, that modern panacea for the ills of widowhood, but ours is a small, inactive community. People suggested this and offered that. Every one had his own pet scheme for helping Enid, but the truth of the matter is, a hunting country is an expensive place in which to bring up and educate three small children.

George had left eight cracking good horses but they had little commercial value. They were clean-bred, first-flight horses on which a master horseman like George could go out front and stay there, but they were useless for the average rider. I have noticed that the better a man rides the less he has to pay for his horses and when any one was found who could ride George's horses, they either had no money or found it unnecessary to go very deep in their pockets to mount themselves.

We were now faced with the inevitable. Enid had put up a tremendously game fight, as she would do, but to no avail, so she had decided to move to town, take a pokey little apartment, and cast in her lot with Sophie Eglinton, who had a shop. For myself I mooned about under the firm conviction that the countryside was to be a much less colorful place with Enid out of it; in that I was reflecting the sentiments of the community as a whole. She was indeed the radiant and dominant note in our countryside.

In all groups of people there are those around whom others naturally congregate. For many years the Ashleys had kept "open house" and much of our social activity had centered around them. It had been our custom to drop into their place at all times of the day and night and always for tea on Sundays. A score or more of cars would be parked in their drive every Sunday. There was never any doubt where we would foregather after a race meet, horse show, hunter trial, or whatever it might be — we automatically headed for the Ashley's to talk it all over, and it was said with truth that there had never been a dull gathering or dinner in their house. If you had week-end guests you were very apt to take them over to meet George and Enid and you felt that they went away with a happier picture of our countryside from having made the visit.

When confronted with the graver problems of life one never failed to take a more sane and hopeful view of things after chatting about them with Enid Ashley. Out of her abundant love for the world and life and people, she gave freely and there was hardly one of us who at some time or another had not been placed under great debt to her. It was because of all this and much more —very much more — that our feelings were so lacerated at the thought of losing her.

For some weeks I had found myself wishing that Colonel

Weatherford had been at home. I hadn't the least idea what he could do in such a situation, but even so I wanted to talk with him, just for the satisfaction that generally followed talking with him about any perplexing problem. He had been in Greece for some months with an English expedition which I understood he had been largely financing and which was said to be excavating some particularly interesting ruins. As he had a way of appearing home quite unexpectedly, I decided to look in at his place to learn whether they had heard anything from him. I was delighted to find from the housekeeper that she had received a message from his man Albert advising her that the Colonel was on the water and expecting to land on Friday.

On Saturday afternoon I was closeted with my old friend in his familiar library, giving him a complete picture of the Ashley matter. At times he could be the most irritating person in the world with whom to talk over such an affair. He had a way of sitting smoking his pipe, to which he would occasionally pay the most minute attention while he apparently paid none to you. Never under any circumstances did his expression undergo any change. I was intensely interested in my subject and could but think of a remark John Drew, the actor, once made to me about the effect that cold, unresponsive audiences have on an actor's performance.

When I finished my recital there was a silence. Of course, I didn't know what part, if any, Enid Ashley might have played in the old man's scheme of things, for he was away a great deal of the time, and seldom went out to tea or dinner; except when he played tennis he was never seen in or about the Club. But still I was hopeful that some constructive suggestion might be forthcoming.

The Colonel arose, took two or three turns of the room with his hands behind his back, and then said: "Pendleton, it's very regrettable, very regrettable. I'm extremely sorry." Then we lapsed into another silence and finally he said, "It has not been my privilege to meet many people comparable to Enid Ashley. I venture to think there are very few. Had you known her mother as I did you would understand the reason." Then to my intense irritation he deliberately changed the subject. Apparently the matter was closed in so far as he was concerned.

I had missed him during his absence and long waited for his return; now that we were reunioning I found myself all out of tune with him and so after one or two futile attempts at conversation I made some excuse to leave him. I knew perfectly well that I was unreasonable, but I had certainly expected something more from him than a bromidic word of regret and a non-productive compliment.

The following Friday dawned as perfect a May day to go a-fishing as that year of grace was apt to furnish, so I set off for Buzzard Hollow stream, deciding to take to the water at Owen Tibbetts' Mill, have luncheon at the big pool above Dent's Crossing, fish the pool and on down the stream during the afternoon, and have my car pick me up at Mellicks' Ford. All told I had a grand morning. By the time I reached the rips just above the big pool I had a very substantial string of fish for our modest waters.

The stream makes a sharp right-hand turn after it passes the rips and then drops into the big pool. I was on the point of wading around some boulders which would have brought me in sight of the pool, when I heard voices. I had antici-pated all morning fishing this fine pool and was disappointed that others had preceded me. As I crawled up the bank and looked through some alders an unexpected thing met my eyes. There on the bank of the pool was Enid Ashley, Enid Ashley's three children, and no less a person than Colonel Weatherford himself. Two of the children were wading, the eldest boy, George, was casting — either fishing or practising. The Colonel was sitting on the ground with his back to me and facing Enid, and was emphatically and energetically expounding something to her. He had a way of making a cup or pocket of his left hand and driving his doubled-up right hand into the cup of his left. This manoeuvre didn't make any noise but gave you the impression of something powerful happening. Enid was looking earnestly and intently at him.

I retreated and walked back up the stream perhaps a quarter of a mile, and sat down on a flat rock for a bit of lunch. Enid Ashley, her three children, John Weatherford, a large picnic lunch, a fire already burning, a mess of fish ready to be cooked and the Colonel driving home some idea with that huge fist of his going like a sledge hammer! This was an interesting sight for a May morning.

I fished all the way back to Owen Tibbetts' and there 'phoned for my car, upon which my man seemed suspicious, thinking no doubt that I had spent the day asleep in Owen's hay mow.

Next day I dropped into Enid's and said, "Enid, I was fishing the Buzzard Hollow Waters yesterday and had my heart set on the 'big pool' but when I reached the pool I found a raft of people and children all over the place, to say nothing of food littered about."

Enid smiled; "Yes I saw you through the alders but I was very much engaged just then."

[60]

"Enid," I said, "perhaps you have guessed that I've been terribly concerned about you and the kiddies, and if what the Colonel was saying to you has any connection with your problems and you would like to tell me I'd indeed like to hear it."

"Pen," she said, "you have been a perfect brick to me, but I can't imagine why you should think that going on a picnic with the Colonel would have any bearing on my problems. He called me up about nine o'clock yesterday and said he wanted to come over to see me. Do you know he is about the only man in the world I'm terrified by? I've known him since I was a wee tot — for as long as I can remember knowing anybody. It was said he was devoted to my mother. It's queer, but whenever I run into him at any sort of a jubilation, a New Year's party, or anything of that kind, I always find him looking at me with such a queer look. I wonder if it hurts him to see my mother's daughter surrounded by people who are a bit care-free. He lives a good deal in the past and has never been in tune with certain modern tendencies. The odd part of it is that I think I am downright fonder of him than almost anybody I know, and yet I practically never see him and don't feel comfortable with him when I do. He is the most genuine person in the world, isn't he?

"I told him I had promised to take the children on a fishing picnic and could not disappoint them. What did he do but ask if he could come along and were we fishing Buzzard Hollow stream and lunching at the big pool. He knew George always fished there. I said yes. So he said he would come. I would have been quite as prepared to hear that the Chief Justice of the United States was coming. And we all met at the pool; we had lunch, the children went off to play and the Colonel and I talked of this and that until it was time to go home, —

and that's about all there was to it." I noticed that when she said, "That's about all there was to it," Enid was not looking at me.

One day about a month later I was stopped by a horse van and asked by the driver to direct him to Mrs. George Ashley's. I told him the way and asked him what he had aboard. "A screw just off the boat from Ireland," he said. The Ashley's place was only half a mile down the road so I turned my car around and followed the van in order to have a look at the Irish horse.

When the van doors were opened and the chute let down a horse walked out that is a bit difficult to describe. It was a dull brown in color and looked as though it stood perhaps 16 hands, yet when you chinned the animal, it measured 16.2 strong. It had lop ears, a decidedly plain head, dull eyes and a listless expression. It was decidedly ewe-necked and ragged over his quarters, the latter accentuated by its being very low in flesh.

As the van man handed the halter shank to Enid's Irish boy, Jimmie, a wry look stole over that experienced boy's face. I asked Jimmie to hold the horse a minute so that I might look at it. Then I concluded it was the plainest, laziest, drollest looking blood horse I have ever set eyes on, but probably the most powerful. I credited it with nine inches of bone and a girth of eighty-two inches. Upon making this reflection I entered my car and as I drove home I kept seeing in my mind's eye a great raking pair of hind quarters that looked as though they could hoist Coeur de Lion in full armor out of the Grand Canyon.

Time went on and Enid Ashley did not move into the stuffy apartment, and Sophie Eglinton's Shop struggled along without her. In a few weeks people ceased asking when Enid was going to town, and the first thing we knew we had forgotten that there had ever been any discussion of her moving away. We continued to drop in at Enid's for tea on Sundays and if possible a few more of us dropped in. To all outward appearances the place looked as of yore. The stables themselves were closed except for one box for *Old Doleful*. Enid's groom, Jimmie, who had been with her since he was a wee shaver and who was conceded to be the best boy in our country, on and with a horse, stayed on and cut the grass, milked the cow, motored the children about and cared for *Doleful*. I noticed that on alternate Sundays self service was inaugurated.

Enid made some very intricate arrangements with the School by which she placed her knowledge of French at the disposal of the School and the School did the same with its facilities for Enid's children. Enid's French stood her in good stead. If you saw a group of cars in front of one of our larger manor houses on any Tuesday afternoon at four o'clock you knew that Enid's class in conversational French was in progress, — twenty-five members at $50 each for the season.

When people said that it was extravagant for Enid to keep *Old Doleful*, she would say, "Oh the old dear isn't mine, you know. He belongs to Colonel Weatherford. I'm just trying to school him for the Colonel. He is such a stupid horse. It seems as though I just never could teach him to jump timber. It seems too dreadful of me to go on charging the Colonel board." I agreed with her, and for the life of me I couldn't understand why, if the Colonel wanted, by such a subterfuge, to lend her something to ride at his expense, he couldn't have picked out an animal that would have been a pleasure to her. He certainly had a stable full.

On the other hand I admired the Colonel's acumen for getting Enid to school a horse for him. A lot of us would have been glad to have had her do the same had we thought of it. She had been making horses ever since she had been in her teens and had a rare knack of giving young horses confidence and making them enjoy jumping. Her first principle was to establish a confidential relationship with a colt and in the accomplishment of this she had endless patience. I have known her to take a young horse fresh from the track, hot, restless and with its nerves on edge, wait two months before mounting it, spend an hour a day leading it about, giving it grass, talking to it, entertaining and amusing it,— and finally when she sensed that the colt's feelings towards her and the world at large were as she wanted them, mount and ride off with no fuss or furor. As a result Enid's horses had exceptional manners and were particularly amenable, no matter how strong the stress of excitement.

Life droned along in our remote world as it was ever wont to do, and finally summer was upon us. Those who spent the winters in town had opened their houses and adopted the country until the close of the hunting season. Those who like myself lived the year around in the country, migrated here and there for a summer vacation. I went up to a snug little harbor in Massachusetts, put my yawl in commission and spent the month of July cruising.

Colonel Weatherford fitted out a sea-worthy craft and with a party of old cronies went up to Labrador to investigate some recently discovered ruins of a very early settlement and to spend long afternoons playing duplicate whist. I was urged to be of the party but had remembrances of games played with those same players at the Union League Club.

I returned about August 15th for the cubbing and to supervise the preparation of a fair sort of horse I was thinking of starting in our Cup Race. This Cup Race of ours is the one event of the year that reminds the outside world that we are still alive. It is an old fixture run over a splendid course and always attracts some very good outside horses.

The Race is not run until October; yet I found no end of excitement about it upon my return. Four or five new horses had arrived in town, all of them racing prospects and some with established reputations. A remarkably good looking horse had arrived from England. The Secretary told me that he had assurances of entries from the very best timber horses then running, and that the event had all the ear-marks of being the best cup race of the series.

A day or two after my return I went over to see Enid and we had a perfectly bully talk. She was cheerful and happy and assured me that she was squeezing through and believed she could make the grade unless floored by some unexpected catastrophe. I asked her if she was still schooling *Old Doleful* for the Colonel and how her conscience was holding out. "Yes," she said, "I am. Isn't it dreadful? The Colonel got away before I had an opportunity to talk to him about it." "Well, Enid," I said, "don't worry. It won't hurt him a bit." In the light of future events I have often recalled how innocent and demure Enid looked as I gave her this advice.

Upon leaving Enid I went in search of Jimmie, from whom I wanted to borrow a twisted snaffle. He was not at the stable, but hearing some hammering going on in a field hidden from view by a wood lot, I walked through the patch of woods to this field, and to my amazement saw a series of new schooling fences — and such fences! The field must have run to thirty acres and was dotted with eight great big stout post and rail fences with the largest top rails I ever saw used in a fence. There was something else that I noticed, namely, that Jimmie didn't seem altogether pleased to see me out in that field, but I put this down to one of the many vexations with which a top rider who has been suddenly converted into a gardener, cowman, chauffeur and nurse must be afflicted.

Jimmie told me he had a bridle such as I wanted and we walked back to the stable. On the way I said, "Jimmie, what in the world are you doing with all those new jumps?" "Why sir," said Jimmie, "Mrs. Ashley was thinking may be perhaps we should be doing a scrap of something about schooling the horse of Colonel Weatherford's. She says as how she can't school it across country no more what with the way he bastes down the farmers' fences. It's himself don't lift any offen the ground when he leps. He leps with his four feet flat on the sod, the varmint. Wasn't it a week now Tuesday that he basted down so many pieces of Mr. Burch's fence that he had no fence at all, at all."

"Jimmie," I said, "you aren't married, are you?" "No sir, praise God." "Well, that's good," I said, "for those are very stout jumps you have built. Have you schooled over them yet?" "Never a ghost of a school," said Jimmie. I took the bridle and departed.

I had rather an odd experience that night. I woke up about two o'clock from a fine, sound, dreamless sleep. I awoke quite suddenly and felt alert and clear minded. My thought reverted to Jimmie and myself standing talking in Enid's thirty-acre field and looking at the nearest of those formidable fences. Lying there in bed I saw something that I had apparently not seen while I was standing with Jimmie. I saw that the turf on both sides of the fence was worn bare. "Never a ghost of a school," Jimmie had said. I found myself sitting up in bed and wondering about this. It also struck me that each and every one of those jumps must have been a good four foot six high. It took me some time to get to sleep again.

September slipped rapidly away and on a Friday evening in early October we were all huddled in the Club dining room for the dinner which always preceded the auctioning of the pool on the Cup Race. It is a convivial occasion except in respect to the dinner one gets, which is atrocious. Kitchen facilities designed to cater to one hundred do service for three hundred. Imported waiters with weird physiognomies deluge the guests and each other with cold and make-shift food. But on the whole people are happy.

I fear I must digress here to interject a bit of local color which has a bearing on this story. The principal topic of conversation at the dinner was the prospects of Emery Brinkley's horse, *Play Leader*, by *Fair Play*, winning the morrow's race. He was the most promising of our local horses that year.

It is not easy to picture our frame of mind towards Brinkley. The very sight of him aroused resentment in certain people.

Brinkley was a broker and it was with him that George Ashley had his account on the fatal day. George had been a great friend and admirer of Brinkley, but there were those who had strong reason for believing that this admiration was not mutual. Brinkley had been an ardent admirer of Enid's long before George appeared on the scene, a situation that does not necessarily promote affection.

[67]

Then George Ashley had been one of the most genuinely loved and respected people on the top side of the earth, and universally admired, while Brinkley was of those who trailed along in the ruck. He was born of a morose disposition and this trailing in the ruck had soured and poisoned his attitude toward the world.

The present bad feeling had been aroused through the assertion of a few fellows who were really "in the know" on the "Street" that the whole thing could have been avoided, and under the circumstances most certainly should have been. This, coupled with the condition in which George's affairs were left, created an undercurrent of very bad feeling.

Brinkley had a great deal of money, even for this day and generation. He inherited a lot and made a lot more through hard work. His interest in sport was genuine, but he lacked a nice sense of the proper thing to do or say at any particular time or place.

Brinkley had purchased the horse *Play Leader* down in Philadelphia for a very long price, very much more of a price than any one in our section ever felt like paying for a timber horse. In a way we regretted this because such horses were sure to "ring down the curtain" on timber racing for ordinary hunters and for owners who could not afford animals of that class. On the other hand Brinkley had properly pointed out that if ours was an open race, there was no sense in letting outside horses come in and gallop all around us, and he was right.

When the room was finally cleared of waiters, old Mr. Dennison, the President of the Club, arose, spoke a word of welcome, and of the object that had brought us together, stated that Judge Bainbridge would auction the pool as he had done for the last eighteen years, and that fifteen percent of the proceeds would go to the National Hunt Servants Fund.

There were fourteen horses in the pool and as the "tops" all had ardent supporters, and the countryside was full of visitors, there was bound to be keen bidding.

Dick Esteys, the Secretary of the Race Committee, announced that the programmes for the Race had arrived from the printer's and would be distributed as an aid to those wishing to bid on the horses. Then he caused every local person in the room, including the Club waiters, to open their mouths, for he continued and said that since the list of entries had been furnished to the newspapers an additional entry had been received and accepted, as would appear in the programme, viz.: Colonel Weatherford's horse, *Mr. Doleful,* who was being ridden by Eric Westmoreland of Virginia.

Enid Ashley was sitting at my table — she was my guest at dinner. She was sitting right opposite to me. I looked at her and must have made a ludicrous appearance in my astonishment, for she put her elbows on the table, rested her chin in her hands and laughed at me in that pleasant, friendly, yet teasing way she has.

Just then Colonel Weatherford came in. He had declined to be a party to relegating so honorable a thing as a man's dinner into a food riot, so he had dined at home and we had arranged to hold a seat for him at our table.

The people around us were on the verge of breaking out into comments on the Colonel's starting that dreary looking brown horse that Enid Ashley had been trying to make jump, but before any one could get started, Judge Bainbridge commenced the auction.

[69]

The first horse sold was a fair entry from Philadelphia. A well bred horse that had won one race at a shorter distance, been placed once or twice, and was being ridden by a well known figure. He was the sort of horse that was very apt to stand up and if the "tops" came to grief, go on and win. An admirer bought his chances for $600. The figure indicated that a good pool was in the making.

The next was an extremely good horse from Maryland that brought $2250. The next three sold for a total of $3300.

Then Judge Bainbridge cleared his throat and said, "The next horse is Mr. Brinkley's *Play Leader*. This horse comes into our country and to this race with a very fine reputation. He is a beautifully bred horse that went the route on the flat, was in the money a number of times over brush, and has won his last two starts over timber. How much am I offered for his chances? Gentlemen, there is $6150 in the pool, and I have seven more horses to sell including this one." A former owner carried him along to $2500. A local syndicate of three went to $3900, Brinkley bought his own horse upon a bid of $4000. And the auction proceeded.

My card showed that when the thirteenth horse had been sold there was $19,600 in the pool.

We had come to the fourteenth and last horse. The Judge picked up his copy of the programme, adjusted his glasses and read the entry to himself. If you have ever been to dinners of this kind you will know that they are exceedingly noisy. There is a holiday feel in the air, and therefore the silence that ensued was the more remarkable. It looked as though everyone in the room was following the Judge's example and reading the entry. When he had finished the Judge removed his glasses, put them in their case, snapped the case, and said, "We now come to the last entry. Our neighbor, Colonel John Weatherford's brown gelding *Mr. Doleful* by *Allepo* out of the French mare *Fayette*. You will note by the star that this is an imported horse. I also note that he is a young horse, five years old." Then he turned toward the Colonel and said: "Colonel Weatherford, we have a very substantial pool for our Race Meet, by far the largest we have ever had. It is difficult for us to appraise a horse but recently arrived in this country, and one which has never started here. Would you be willing, Sir, to say a word respecting your horse?"

The Colonel reared his six feet two out of his diminutive camp chair. He looked resplendent in his scarlet dress coat. He was a great old crank about his linen and appointments. Albert was forever sending his waistcoats and shirts to some French woman in New York to be laundered, but his care bore fruit; there was a pleasing immaculateness about him.

He complimented the Judge on his achievement in extracting $19,000 from the audience and then delivered himself of the following rather baffling remarks:

"My entry in tomorrow's race is, I believe, the most unsightly horse ever entered in a timber race in this or any other country. His appearance speaks for itself. This is his first race here or abroad. A man in Ireland told me he might make a race horse. I thought he would, so I bought him and paid a good price for him. He has been schooled, trained and handled for me by Mrs. Ashley. Whereas he has never been so much as galloped in company with other horses in this country, yet Mrs. Ashley encourages me by saying that he has shown well when in company with her grey lead pony. Under the circumstances I do not feel free to encourage any one to wager on the horse in his first race. On the other hand, as long as you have asked me to speak about the horse I would not wish any one to feel later on that I had belittled him, and so I repeat that I thought very well of him in Ireland, well enough to pay a substantial price for him, and I give it as my opinion that should he succeed in standing up tomorrow he may beat a horse or two and perhaps some that are apparently well considered."

The Colonel was about to sit down when Brinkley was seen rising to his feet. "Colonel," he said, "you have remarked that should your horse manage to stand up you think he will beat some horses that are pretty well considered. Could I interest you in a little side bet?" It was just like Brinkley — exactly like him. He disliked the Colonel, who, he thought, was forever slighting him.

What the Colonel started to say in reply I don't know, but I saw him make a change of front. I detected something going on in his mind, and he said in his most honeyed voice, "Mr. Brinkley, perhaps we should let the Judge finish auctioning off the last horse; then I should be delighted to discuss your suggestion further."

"How much am I offered for *Mr. Doleful*," asked the Judge. There was not a sound. Frankly, after the Colonel's statements it was difficult to appraise the horse's chances. There was $19,600 in the pool and fourteen starters. Thirteen might fall down and stay down and leave *Mr. Doleful* the sole survivor. Finally some one said $250. Then it went by slow stages to $400 and stuck there. Then I heard the Colonel's voice ring out clear and decisively: "I will bid $600 for Mrs. Ashley."

You could have heard a pin drop. There was no other bid.

[72]

He didn't say $410 for Mrs. Ashley. He thought they would stop bidding as soon as they heard her name and he didn't want it too cheap. He didn't want to tackle Brinkley before the horse was sold because he feared that if he took Brinkley for a ride it might send the horse up in the pool to an unwarrantable price. He detested Brinkley. If he hadn't, nothing in the world would have caused him to get up in front of a lot of people and do what he did. He could have transacted the matter in private, but he seemed anxious to treat with Brinkley in front of the whole countryside. So he said, "Mr. Brinkley, I interrupted you a moment ago only because I thought the Judge might like to finish his labors. You said something about a side bet. Perhaps I exposed myself by some over-confidence in my horse. What have you in mind? I assume you are not contending that the chances of the two horses are by any means equal."

Brinkley replied, "I will wager you that my horse navigates more fences than your horse without falling and that if they both stand up my horse wins. I will concede that my horse is favored through greater experience but any horse is apt to fall at even the first fence. I will lay you $1000 to $500, or if you would like to make it a real wager it suits me."

It was very evident that Brinkley had been celebrating. Nothing of this kind had ever happened in public in the Club House, and I saw old Mr. Dennison, the President of the Club, start to his feet. Weatherford also saw him and without a second's hesitancy he said, "Well let us make it ten thousand to five."

There are a lot of quiet, garden-loving, home-staying, delightful people in our countryside who come regularly to these dinners, yet know comparatively little about what is going on, and the room buzzed with questions and explanations of what had happened.

Enid's face was a study. Her's had been the sole responsibility for getting the horse ready — a young horse — green at timber and the dreariest looking nag in three kingdoms. She had schooled and conditioned him in a back field and with no means of really trying him.

The party broke up. Enid shook hands all around and I went with her to find her car. As I was putting her in I said, "Enid, do you suppose the old man is beginning to let go?— You know what I mean." "I don't know," she said. "Let us wait until tomorrow, but Pen, have you stopped to think what that pool would do for my kiddies? When you haven't anything in the world those figures stagger one. I've done everything I know how to do for that horse; no matter what happens Eddie and I have done our best. I wish it was all over. My head is splitting." I closed the car door and she drove off.

Saturday dawned a perfect racing day and I had every reason to enjoy that particular Cup Race. I had scratched my own entry, an uncertain performer at best, who had filled a tendon after his last school, and free from the concerns incidental to ownership, I should have felt as free as a lark. Instead I was sunk with depression. The Colonel's untimely wager, the amount at stake in the pool for Enid, my complete mistrust of *Mr. Doleful*, preyed upon my mind. Although I had been told nothing I now sensed that Enid's scheme of things was in some way dependent upon this young Irish horse accomplishing what certainly appeared to me to be the impossible.

Upon reaching the course I felt disinclined to chatter and

so walked off by myself to watch the horses come from the stable to the saddling paddock. I was standing thus and watching four or five horses which included Brinkley's impressive chestnut and *Mr. Doleful*, when of a sudden there was an exclamation back of me excelling in violence anything I have ever heard in my life. This was followed by a stout Irish voice—"It's himself — the ugly varminty lop-eared brute. It's not another there could be the likes of him." I turned and to my astonishment recognized the portly figure of Mr. Timothy McManus Delaney of County Cork, Ireland.

The owner of this voice and author of these refined comments was standing with his mouth ajar, his massive purple cheeks puffed out and his small blue eyes fairly dancing. He was following *Mr. Doleful's* progress with absorbing interest. Upon recognizing me there was another vehement explosion, much hand shaking and an equal amount of calling upon one and several of the saints to bear witness to this and that.

Mr. Delaney was visiting his son who had come to America some years ago, and who, from having started as a whipper-in to a famous pack of hounds was now marketing finished hunters to a fashionable clientele and doing extremely well. The son was showing his worthy sire an American timber race. I had first gone to Mr. Delaney in Ireland many years ago and he had indeed "done" me very well. I owed much of the success of my first hunting trip in his country to him.

No one could question Mr. Delaney's affability, yet he was primarily a man of business, so he went to the bottom of the reunion business with the greater dispatch. Then he looked about him and seeing himself surrounded by a group of on-lookers attracted by his 18 stone, checked suit, and phenomenal expanse of gold watch chain, he drew me to one side. "Mr. Pendleton, Sir, did you see the ugly heathen go by a minute sinst — the ugly mug of him." He then looked about him cautiously and continued in a low tone. "Do you know him? — No you don't — how would you — but I do. It's in a bit of a hurry I'm in, Mr. Pendleton. Now would there be a lad here at this fair making a book — a lad mind you that could be found after the race this side of your Misupi River. Would you be taking me to him," upon saying which the old worthy reached down, took a tight hold of his balloon-like trousers with his right hand, inserted his left hand into a cavern-like pocket until half of his forearm had disappeared, and extracted a roll of bills that, if it would not have choked the proverbial bull, would have made him cough. He then untied the red tape with which the mass was tied, extracted two one-hundred-dollar bills which he solemnly raised to his lips and kissed; then he deposited them in his checked waistcoat pocket, returned the roll to his pocket, hit the turf a whack with his stick, and said: "Now let us find the lad."

"Mr. Delaney," I said, "this Race will not be called for twenty minutes. Now then, out with it. Tell me the whole story." "Hist," he said, "come away. We will sit a spell on the wall yonder." When we were ensconced on the stone wall with no one within even shouting distance he whispered, "Sure it's O'Connor's colt himself I'm telling you. Wasn't it raised next to me. Didn't my boy, Dennis, break him? Didn't he gallop him? Didn't he school him a time or two? Didn't they try him afore it was decent light alongside o' my horse that won the Dunkhollow Stakes? Mr. Pendleton, it's

fifty years I've been buying, selling, breeding, racing, training and schooling horses, it is, and there was never a lump of
a horse bred in Ireland with a bigger lep nor one that could
lep faster and land more going away, and man, oh man, the
Divil himself couldn't throw him down. He can hit a fence
that hard a lad can't sit a-top of him what with the jolt of it
but he won't turn over. And did you ever seen him move?—
the ugly clout. He runs without trying. He does.

"And what does that low heathen, O'Connor, do but sell
him afore ever we had a chance to slip him into an easy berth.
The pity on it. Why there was no one knew of the horse only
O'Connor and me and Dennis and the lads on the place.
Wasn't it myself said to O'Connor —'O'Connor,' I says, 'the
looks of him should be worth a million sterling to us what
with the odds we should get on him,' and I says to myself, 'It
will be retiring I will after O'Connor's colt starts.' And one
day O'Connor comes to my place and says, 'I'm after selling
that lop-eared colt.' I'd as soon believed he'd sold his old
woman. And I says, 'And what would you be doing that for?'
And he says, 'Would you look at this,' and he showed me a
draft for 3000 pounds, and the horse had niver even had a
look at a starter. 'He goes to America,' he says, 'and I wish
him luck.' 'Well, O'Connor,' I says, 'You sold the best Grand
National prospect in Ireland today.' That's what I says to
him, Mr. Pendleton. Now maybe he don't know how to lep
these slivers of fences of yours, and maybe he ain't as fit as
he should be — maybe not — but no matter, no matter. It
will take a tirrible horse to bate him. That it will."

I extracted two hundred dollars from my less pretentious
roll and Mr. Delaney and I climbed the slope to where the
bookmakers were doing a thriving business. I pointed out

three members of the profession with whom I had had satisfactory transactions in the past and stood aside to watch the old veteran in operation. Wagering at our Cup Races is rather a mild performance. The amounts wagered are quite modest. They are mostly ten dollar bets, a few fifties, and now and then a hundred.

Mr. Delaney approached the first slate and read through the quotations. Then I heard him say, "Now then, my lad, I'm just over from Ireland. I don't know any of these horses. Is there any horse from God's country that would be running?" Some one piped up, "Mr. Thomas's horse, *Beck's Boy* is an Irish horse. He's just over and cost a lot of money." "Did he?" said Mr. Delaney. "And what's his odds?" The talent quoted the horse. "It's no go," said Mr. Delaney. "If I'm going to bet I want some odds. Would there be another Irish horse?" A boy said, "Colonel Weatherford's nag — the one with the funny ears and Roman nose — he's Irish," and there was a laugh. "Is he?" said Mr. Delaney. "He don't sound so hopeful now, does he? What's his price and what's his name?" The bookie looked up at his slate and pointed to *Mr. Doleful* 9 to 1. "What, 9 to 1 for that horse? Well it looks to me like you lads are afeared of all these nags. I'm thinking a week in Ireland would do you a lot of good."

"How much were you calculatin' to play, governor?" said the bookie. "Well, I didn't exactly know," answered Delaney, "I was thinking may be a pound or two or may be more if I could get some decent odds. They tell me it's a bad course and a likely lot of horses running." "Well," said the bookie, "Let's have a hundred, governor, and I'll give you a chance to win an even thousand." Mr. Delaney extracted his two hundred dollars, separated them, handed one to the maker of the book, held the other in his hand, and contemplated it. The bookmaker and his assistant went into a huddle and I saw the Irishman's eyes riveted on them. Then the bookie said, "If you'd like to make it two, governor, I'd be glad to accommodate you." And Mr. Delaney's second hundred went the way of the first. I transacted my affair elsewhere and then went to the paddock to have a look at the horses, which were just starting for the post. My interest in and hopes for *Mr. Doleful* had most certainly mounted.

He had taken his place well down towards the end of the line, and was standing with his head down, his eyes half closed and his listless ears draped over the sides of his head. Again my faith wavered. Young Westmoreland waved me a cheerful salutation which I dolefully attributed to the misplaced optimism of youth and the horses started for the post with my old grey mare, *Lady Echo*, done up in red bandages with white cotton showing top and bottom, leading the way. Feeling irritable, I detested red bandages on white horses at race meets. As I walked along I saw the Colonel's Albert circulating among the bookmakers and knew the Colonel was getting in some of his fine work; I was glad Mr. Delaney and I had consummated our arrangements before Albert commenced.

I saw Enid and the Colonel walking ahead of me and joined them and we selected a point of vantage on which to see the thing through.

There may have been better fields of horses entered in cross country events in this country but I for one never saw or read of one. It was indeed a brilliant group of jumpers that faced the starter that mellow October-day for our Cup Race. They had foot and courage and were bred to jump and stay. They had been trained by men to whom training was a well-learned art and they were being ridden by the best amateurs the country had to offer. In addition to all this they were to race over as sweet a bit of American landscape as could be found in a year's search.

As I watched the horses lined up and saw the starter holding his flag high above his head I made an effort to shake off my sense of anxiety and so enjoy the spectacle, but it was plain that the amount at stake for the game little woman beside me kept me from really enjoying the race.

I heard the Colonel ask Enid what, if any, instructions she had given Eric Westmoreland and heard her say, "I told him that there was just one thing I cared about and that was to keep my horse out of and away from the crowd — I told him that if he ever let that youngster get mixed up with falling horses or refusing horses or riderless horses or people strewn all over the ground, his winning smile and southern voice wouldn't save him from what I would do and say to him. Colonel, I don't care what they do to the horse — what all of them do to him, if they only give him room to jump. He doesn't know enough yet to jump all hedged in. A lot of those boys out there are great fun to dance with, but during the last half mile they know a lot of tricks. They are all open and above-board about it, but they are not intent on helping each other. Oh, I do wish they would start."

Then the flag dropped.

For the first mile it looked as though every one was trying to lay off the pace. Two horses had gone down at the third fence, but the rest of the field were running well together — all except the brown horse who was last and with lots of room between himself and the field. So far he had fenced faultlessly but every time he jumped Enid's right foot came off the ground. She was living with her horse every single inch of that long, perilous journey. From time to time a horse would go down, and there were the usual dangers from loose horses dodging about. During these tense moments I saw Enid's hand pressed hard against her cheek.

At the end of two and a half miles seven horses were left and (as seldom happens) the survivors happened to be the "tops." Eric was still keeping by himself. If things continued as they were then going we were certain of a rough and tumble finish at the end.

This thought may have struck Sheldon Edwards who was riding Brinkley's horse, for at the three-mile point he commenced to draw away but Jerry Hadfield, on *The Philander,* a crack Philadelphia entry, accepted the challenge and they raced forward together. It was evident that the rest of the field thought the pace too rich or hoped the leaders would come back to them, for no one gave chase. I stole a glance at Enid. Her mouth had a tight, set expression and there were fleeting twitches at the corners. Two exceptionally fast and brilliant horses were well out front and racing on; four high-class horses were between the brown horse and the leaders.

Enid said, "He can't wait any longer. He mustn't; he mustn't; he must go up." The Colonel took his pipe out of his mouth, knocked the ashes out of it against his stick, and remarked, "That boy's a chip off the old block. The minute he is over the next fence he will come through." They were over it and he came through. The brown horse had no sooner landed over that fence than Eric shot him forward and before the four riders in front of him knew what was happening the brown had slipped by them and was giving chase to the leaders. I heard a great sigh and heard Enid say, "Now we *will* go racing," and heard the Colonel mutter to himself, "D——n good boy. Blood will tell. Go a long way, that boy."

Enid had said, "We will go racing," and I'll tell you we did. *Play Leader* and *Philander* were running neck and neck while Eric was holding his horse three lengths in the rear. Of a sudden I heard the Colonel's stick hit the ground and heard him break out, "That boy doesn't know those two horses. He hasn't been close enough to them to know what they have left. He can't risk it any longer. That *Fair Play* horse is a bulldog." As he was speaking the horses took the third jump from the last and no sooner had they landed than Eric moved up. "Good boy," murmured the Colonel, "Good boy."

The brown horse was now running neck and neck with the other two. There had never been such a contest in the twenty-six years of our Cup Race. Ten thousand people on the hillside were silent in suspense. The strain was telling on Enid, and I could not look at her. "Oh, Colonel what should he do — what would you do?" she asked. "I'd sit still," said the Colonel. They were headed for the last fence and you couldn't have told which horse was in front. Never before that day nor since have I seen horses driven so completely wide open at four-foot timber, and as those three great clean-bred horses came flying towards that last and so vital fence, Enid Ashley made a comment that was indeed prophetic and rang in my ears for a long time afterwards. The horses were not above a dozen strides from this last fence when she said, "There is only one horse in this race that has an even chance of standing up at timber going that fast and that's my horse."

Mr. Doleful goes on to win.

The next moment there were two of the most terrific and spectacular falls ever seen in the history of racing, and a low-headed, sombre, lop-eared, doleful brown horse went on to win.

When I turned around to speak to Enid she had reached her right hand up to the Colonel's shoulder, taken a hold of the lapel of his coat with her left hand, and pressed her forehead against his chest. You don't have to see a person cry to know what they are doing, and the Colonel was looking down at her with a kindly twinkle in his fine gray eyes.

I thought it best to leave them together and so I walked on down the hill. I know it will sound a bit braggadocio but for the moment I had forgotten all about the bookmaker. That race was something more than just a horse race for me. As I started over to have a look at the winner, I saw ahead of me a large man in a checked suit stoop forward, then I saw him extract something from his pocket, untie it, add something to it, raise it to his lips, re-deposit it in his pocket, take a good grip of his stick and waddle on. This reminded me of something very important to which I immediately attended.

The ensuing hours were occupied in the usual rounds of visits and festivities which immediately follow any stirring event.

Later in the evening, as I arrived at the Hunt Ball, I overtook Enid going up the steps just in front of me. "Pen," she said, "I have been looking for you ever since the race. Wherever I went they said you had just left. I want to talk to you ever so much. Find a quiet corner on the porch and I will be right out."

When we were on the porch she opened her bag and handed me a folded piece of paper and said, "Read it." I did so.

Dear Enid:

I hand you my check for $26,928.50 in conformity with our agreement. A statement is attached. You have put me under obligation to you through the happy outcome of this venture.

Affectionately,

JOHN WEATHERFORD.

I turned to the statement and read:

Disbursements

Cost of brown horse.........	$ 3,000.00
Transportation, etc.	283.00
Paid to you for board........	810.00
Insurance, van hire, etc.	190.00
Total	$ 4,283.00

Receipts

By sale of horse today to Mr. Van Elder for $12,000 (your ½ of net profits)	$ 3,858.50
½ of $10,000 rec'd. from Mr. Brinkley	5,000.00
Club pool less $600..........	16,570.00
½ of my winnings	1,500.00
	$26,928.50

I handed the check and statement back to Enid and she put them in her bag.

"Pen," she said, "isn't he a knight errant? The agreement didn't read quite like that but he insists he won't have it any other way. Twenty-seven thousand dollars!"

I was trying to place Mr. Van Elder when I suddenly recalled an anaemic young man with a drooping blond mustachio who came up to the country once a month from the Colonel's bank in New York to go over the Colonel's accounts with him.

Then Eric Westmoreland came up and Enid started to go off with him, but came back to me to say, "Pen, don't you think the Colonel is the greatest buyer in the world? Think of buying a horse for $3,000 and selling him for $12,000!" "Yes, Enid," I said, "he is a wonderful buyer," and as I watched her and Eric having their dance of victory together, I thought of the $15,000 draft Mr. O'Connor had deposited in his bank in the County Cork.

CHAPTER VI.

Mary Sedgwick's Hunt Team

OUR annual horse show is no better than and, except in one respect, no different from any one of a dozen other shows. The difference is the fuss and furor we make over one very important event — our hunt team class, and there is a lot of fuss and more furor. By four o'clock in the afternoon of the show all other classes are supposed to have been judged and to be out of the way and the balance of the day is given over to the hunt teams.

The class is shown over a hilly outside course of a mile and a half dotted with fourteen semi-natural fences. One of the conditions calls for horses to be shown at a pace comparable to "a fast twenty-minute burst to hounds." To be on the winning team and have one's name engraved on the permanent trophy which has hung in the club house for eighteen years has become a fetish with some of our younger contingent, and the rivalry is very keen. People commence long before the show to make up their teams and there is much getting together for practice and earnest discussion pertaining to items of appointment. The class is a boon to the tailors and a drag on paternal pocketbooks.

For the two previous years the trophy had been won by a team of three girls: Phyllis Newcombe, Audrey Emerson and little Mary Sedgwick, our Rector's daughter. The event had never before been won by the same team for two successive years, and as a result the three girls, their horses and their riding were clothed with local glamour.

The first two girls were of the much-photographed and written-up class of débutantes, and I could hardly blame the youthful photographers who were forever snapping them, for they were exceedingly good to look upon. For young ladies credited by the press with doing the multitude of things which the press said they did and being in the countless places they were reputed to be in, they rode extremely well; to do them justice they went like nailers to hounds. They had courage and sublime confidence in themselves and their horses. Of hunting the fox they knew nothing and cared less, which a tolerant and long suffering M.F.H. said was probably a blessing in disguise.

Little Mary Sedgwick was of a very different type. She was a small wisp of a girl — sensitive to a fault, and retiring, but a great favorite with the older people. She was a dreamy little person who went through life with never a thought of her personal appearance and looked it. Her hair was forever askew, and if she wore a garment possessed of a collar it was sure to be half up and half down, and there was no one else's hunting stock in the length and breadth of the land that could work itself into such a muss.

Mary played the best game of tennis of any woman in the club and in my opinion knew more about the science of fox hunting, in spite of her eighteen years, than any woman who hunted with us, and, excepting only Enid Ashley, she rode better than any woman in our countryside.

I admit that when one looked upon Phyllis Newcombe and Mary Sedgwick one saw two very different pictures, but for myself I enjoyed watching Mary with her lithe, unconscious stride swinging across the club grounds. She had the gayest of smiles and when she smiled at you you knew it came from the heart. One day as she walked by us smiling and waving her hand, Colonel Weatherford said, " 'Pippa Passes'. Of course, Pendleton, all may not be well with the world but Mary Sedgwick certainly makes me think it is."

Mary had been taken into the now famous hunt team only because she happened to own a very workmanlike chestnut horse. Colonel Weatherford had bought it at Melton Mowbray a few seasons before, at a long price, but finding or pretending to find it not up to his weight had sold him for a song to the rector for Mary to hunt, although there were a dozen people who would have gladly paid much money to get the animal. It was not of the show type but a knowledgeable judge would have had trouble faulting it in the conformation of a workmanlike hunter and it was a consistent performer.

It so happened that I sat next to Mary's mother an evening or so after the team had won. Mrs. Sedgwick knew of my affection for Mary and spoke of certain things connected with the aftermath of the hunt team class that were perplexing to one having no knowledge of such matters. She told me that Mary would not eat any dinner after the event but went to her room; that when, later in the evening, Mrs. Sedgwick had gone in to see her she had found Mary in bed, with the pillow and Mary's cheeks very damp.

Mrs. Sedgwick is one of the most understanding persons I know, with a heart large enough to serve a dozen ordinary people; it seems mother and daughter had the most unburdening talk that had passed between them in many years. Mrs. Sedgwick and I had been friends for a very long time and she told me how it had come to light that Mary was an extreme hero-worshipper — how she considered Phyllis Newcombe and Audrey Emerson the very acme of everything she herself would have liked to be and how in comparison with them she considered herself a poor, drab, untidy, insignificant person; that riding in the hunt team with those two divinities had been Mary's crowning achievement and the winning of the event her supreme moment. The reaction which followed had been rather severe.

One hot Saturday afternoon I was sitting on our club porch with Colonel Weatherford. We had just finished a hotly contested old man's tennis match with Mr. Dennison and Judge Bainbridge, and as we had finally defeated our opponents the Colonel was in a prime humor. The other two had gone off in search of their respective wives, detouring en route, as the Colonel said, into the locker-room bar.

As I was ordering tea I heard some people come up on the porch and sit down back of us, recognizing the dulcet voices of Phyllis Newcombe and Audrey Emerson. Phyllis said, "Have you heard about Margery Hadfield's new horse? You haven't? Oh, my dear! Wait till you see it. It's a bright chestnut with three white legs and white on its face and it's been winning everything everywhere. As soon as I heard about it I went straight over to see Margery and we have our hunt team all fixed up for the show next month. You, Margery and I, and what a team!"

"Wonderful," Audrey said, "When can we get in a school? Do you suppose we would have time to get three shad-belly coats made? They're so different and I think they're terribly swank. Come on, let's go over to Margery's right now and talk it all over. By the way what about Mary Sedgwick?

You'll have to say something to her. You told her we would have the same team, and I know she has been schooling that common old crock of hers for a month."

"What a pest," said Phyllis. "I suppose I'll have to tell her, as the team will be entered in my name. I'll certainly be glad to be shut of her. Will you ever forget trying to get her dressed — that awful habit; and borrowing a silk hat for her — and the struggle we had getting a hunting veil on her — and that awful hair of hers! She is a perfect nightmare."

Just then I saw Mary coming up the club steps. Phyllis Newcombe also saw her and went over to her and as they talked I saw a deep flush spread over Mary's face; I make no bones of the fact that there was a flush on my face but from a different emotion. I had entirely forgotten that Colonel Weatherford was sitting anywhere near me and was decidedly surprised to hear his voice — "Pendleton, it's a flinty world. A d—— flinty world."

One morning about two weeks later I was called to the 'phone and found it to be Colonel Weatherford who wanted to know if I could come over to his place the following afternoon at four o'clock and would I pull on a pair of jodphurs. I promised to come, concluding that the Colonel wanted me to throw a leg over some new horse he had purchased. When I arrived they told me the Colonel was out in the schooling field. Upon reaching the field I saw some horses with tack on and a woman riding side saddle, whom I finally recognized as Mary Sedgwick.

The Colonel came up and said, "Pendleton, I have entered a hunt team in the horse show. We three are going to ride. You'll do it, won't you? I know you detest shows but not more than I do. I haven't ridden in one for thirty years. I would very much appreciate it if you would ride." Reluctantly, very reluctantly, I agreed. The Colonel riding in a hunt team at a horse show in scarlet during mid-summer was something difficult for one to grasp. I had literally to concentrate my mind on the project before I could feel confident that I was not suffering from the effect of the then existing hot wave.

"All right," said the Colonel. "That's fine. Now then Jimmie, give Mr. Pendleton a leg up on *John Mistletoe*. I am riding *Athelstone* and Mary has her own horse." As we started to move off the Colonel drew me to one side and said, "We must act and look as keen as mustard in front of Mary. Now don't forget. Heads up and all that sort of thing. It will be a hideous affair but we can see it through." We had our school — the first of six or seven — and I discovered that when the Colonel said a school he meant a school.

In Mary's estimation there were two supermen in our countryside. One, the M. F. H. because he symbolized the institution and sport to which Mary was so devoted. The other was Colonel Weatherford. The Colonel was a great friend of her father, and whenever he was at their house Mary would sit and fix her eyes on him and drink in his every word. His size, appearance, voice and decisive delivery seemed to entrance her. His every comment and observation were as the pronouncement of an oracle.

The Colonel entered upon the business of this hunt team with all the thoroughness with which he would have prepared to campaign a string of race horses and Mary's seriousness as we went through with these interminable schools finally had its effect upon me; I found myself planning and cogitating upon how I could best contribute to the success of the venture.

MARY SEDGWICK'S HUNT TEAM

The momentous day finally arrived and it was hot beyond belief. The Colonel and I dressed in the club house. I had a bad enough time but nothing comparable to the Colonel. His man Albert was shedding buckets. The locker-room was filled with golfers who gaped at the performance. Our scarlet coats seemed to weigh a ton and were gruesome to the touch. As I was adjusting my stock for the third time and noticing how wilted and crinkled it had become under the chin I heard a fat little man say to his neighbor, "It was 92 at three o'clock." By the time the Colonel's stock was tied to his liking his face was purple, yet his eye was alert to every detail. He looked closely at my stock and even gave it a pull or two and then, discovering that our gold safety pins did not match, directed Albert to hunt about and equip him with one of the proper size. We waddled out of the locker-room with our silk hats on — our hat-guards flapping behind us, heavy buckskin gloves on perspiring hands, while a dozen golfers jeered at us from the shower room, and Eddie Templeton sent a lugubrious looking locker boy after us with two towels and talcum powder, with Mr. Templeton's compliments. The Colonel strode grimly on towards the women's dressing room. As we mounted the stairs he turned and said: "God willing, I shall finance Mary to Europe this time next year."

Upon reaching the dressing room he asked the maid in a voice that frightened her half to death whether Mrs. Ashley and Miss Sedgwick were within and upon being told that they were, sent word that it was time to get mounted. Mary appeared followed by Enid Ashley who had been serving as lady's maid.

After the picture I have drawn of poor little Mary Sedgwick I wish you might have seen her as she walked out of that dressing room. For as long as I could remember she had been wearing a re-fitted habit of Enid Ashley's. Today she was resplendent. I didn't sense the whole story at first for I hadn't heard that Eugène, the Colonel's chauffeur, had taken Enid and Mary to town any number of times to the best habit-maker in New York, and to the Colonel's boot-maker and hatter. And let me tell you that when Enid Ashley took a hand at turning any one out to ride in an appointment class, that person was turned out; and when Enid put the finishing touches to any one's hair and adjusted and tied a hunting veil, the wearer of that veil could conquer empires.

It can hardly be said of our community that we are smart — whatever that much used word may mean, — and in the forty-odd years of our hounds we had never seen a woman turned out in a shad-belly coat until Mary appeared in one that day, and no other woman wore one that year in spite of the conversation I had heard on the club porch.

Enid lined us up for a final inspection. There we were — two scarlet and one black shad-belly coats — three cream colored double breasted waistcoats with two rows of three small gold hunt buttons showing below each coat, three very beautifully ironed hats, and one new all black hat-guard and two black ones with a single gold do-dad attached — and our crops matched and so did the thongs and snappers and I don't know what else.

You had only to see Mary walk across a tennis court in her ordinary garb to sense that in spite of everything she wore being at sixes and sevens she had a decidedly distinctive air and personality and now with everything at sixes — with all the talent in the land lavished upon her and with the poise of a long line of distinguished Sedgwicks back of her she was nothing short of superb. Confound it, I'm too old — a lot too old to have my heart go pitter patter about eighteen-year-old Mary Sedgwick, but if it didn't go pitter patter I don't know what it did go, and the fact that the fluttering was paternal has nothing to do with the situation.

We started for the ring — Mary in the center and we two six-footers striding along on each side while Mary's diminutive new boots which the Colonel's boot boy had worked on for two days pattered and twinkled to keep pace with us. As I was on the point of putting Mary up, Enid admonished, "Now Mary don't forget. You mustn't touch your hat or your stock or your veil or take your gloves off and if the veil makes your nose itch remember the itch will go away in time of its own accord. Here's good luck," and she kissed Mary before I put her up. The Colonel said, "Mary, that's not a patch on what I'm going to do to you when we win this class, for God bless me if you're not the best looking woman I've seen since Queen Alexandra's day."

If there were ever three horses and three sets of tack perfectly turned out in this country, they were turned out for us that day. The Colonel's stable and tack room were always referred to in our country as models and it had been a source of keen disappointment to his boys at horse show time that the Colonel would never exhibit his horses, — so the stable had spread itself for this event. Old Pat Dwyer, in charge of the stable, who had been with the Colonel for forty-two years, was in a state bordering on complete flux. Eddie Walsh, Tom Murphy, and two other boys whose names I could never remember, goaded by the old man's exhortations, were sissing and rubbing everything in sight and when we were finally mounted Pat set them to dusting off our boots and snatching a cloth from one of the boys whom he reviled as a lazy varmint, he gave the Colonel's left boot such a trouncing that the Colonel accused him of bringing on a cramp.

When all that could be done for us had been done and we were about to start for the gate I saw and heard something I was not meant to see or hear. Old Pat Dwyer, on the pretext of having a last look at the balance strap on Mary's saddle pressed a small bit of gray fur into her hand and I heard him say, "Slip it in your pocket for me, Miss Mary, but mind now don't mention it to the boss. He laughs at sich things, but it's myself has a power o' faith in 'em. And God help you to win for us, Miss Mary."

When we reached the gate Phyllis Newcombe's team was standing at the head of the line. Back of them was a good looking bay team from a neighboring hunt, then a gray team I did not recognize, then ourselves. The gate was opened — a man looked at the number on Phyllis's back and called through a megaphone to the Judges, "Number 11, Number 11 now jumping" and the class was on.

From where we stood we had a good view of the course, and those three chestnut thoroughbreds hadn't gone above a dozen paces before I reluctantly admitted that if they performed as well as they looked they would be unbeatable. I watched them go down to the first fence and jump it evenly and perfectly. I watched them do the same at the fourteenth and every fence in between. They went at a fine bold hunting pace and preserved perfect spacing. When they had finished the crowd burst into spontaneous applause as well it might. During the performance Mary had been standing up in her stirrup with her eyes focused on the three girls. There was no way of telling what was going on in her mind but when the last horse was safely over the fence she whispered to me: "I don't suppose anything in the world could beat that. I feel ever so bad, Mr. Pendleton, about all these things," pointing to her habit. "They cost the Colonel, oh, such a terrible lot of money! I didn't want him to do it and mother didn't, only he said he had wanted to show in this class for years and years and that my horse was the only one that would go with his and oh, I did want him to win it so badly and now it all seems wasted. Do you think he will feel very badly?"

The two teams in front of us made workmanlike performances and then it was our turn. The Colonel adjusted his hat, settled his 210 pounds down in the saddle, squared his shoulders and went through the gate with Mary following him, with me in the rear, — and we went to work. The first jump was a four-foot post-and-rail fence which you approached down a slight slope. The Colonel always rode with fine determination and with his heart well over a fence before he arrived at it, and therefore his horses did the same and jumped clean and courageously with him. I had never thought to gain a thrill out of riding in a hunt team, yet I admit experiencing a sense of exhilaration as we went down to that fence. Before it was my turn to jump I saw the Colonel's great shoulders well on in front and *Athelstone* striding up the next slope. That *Athelstone* horse of his was a monstrous animal with a terrific stride and iron determination. I never saw a horse of his size and weight that was so active and alert. He could turn on a ten-cent piece and it took a strong rider to pilot him for the first half hour on a cold windy morning. The Colonel had paid thirteen hundred guineas for him in England.

I never felt greater admiration and affection for the Colonel than I did that day. There he was in his great thick scarlet coat galloping over a mile-and-a-half course on a steaming day, mounted on his best horse and I on one rated practically as good, both of them having been taken up from pasture only because of this class — and all to make a Roman holiday for a friend's little girl whose heart and feelings had been hurt.

I don't know how we looked to others, or what sort of a performance we appeared to be putting up, but what I do know is that not one of our horses laid a toe to one of those fourteen stiff jumps, that the distance between us never varied a dozen feet, that we rode at a real hunting pace, that our horses dropped their heads and looked at their fences and jumped them in good, workmanlike form, that not a horse took more than a pleasant hold of the bit, that the Colonel and I were on two 17-hand horses and Mary on one 16.2, that each horse had a bit of white on his face, that their manes were braided and tails pulled and trimmed as only Pat Dwyer knew how to do such things, and finally that these horses had been selected by the Colonel in England and Ireland after years of search, with him credited with being one of the best judges in America.

When the sixteen teams had performed, we all rode over to the regular horse show ring and lined up for the judging of conformation and appointments. We were a trifle late, through waiting for Alfred to procure a bottle of mineral water for the Colonel, and as a result took our place at the bottom of the line. The judges commenced their tortuous inspection, noting the numbers on the riders' backs and consulting their cards and making notes thereon. They finally reached us — looked us over and withdrew to compare notes and discuss the matter of awards.

It is not of my making or ordering if judges as they warm

to their work talk so that certain exhibitors can overhear them. There were two judges, Campbell Duncan and young Taylor Henderson. I heard Henderson say, "Well, Duncan, I've about finished. There were five clean performances, but the three blood horses ridden by the girls win by a block. Then I should think that nice brown team No. 7 should be second, and I don't care much how the third and fourth go. There were a lot of bully performances. The gray team ridden by some hunt staff put up a fine show, and then that team down at the end of the line went clean, but I wouldn't own such a flock of giraffes. I'd need a ladder to get up on them. What are your ideas?" And Duncan said, "Well, Henderson, I understand these people attach a lot of importance to this event and I don't blame them. It's the best hunt team class I've ever seen in my life. I would like to make sure that we are right. We have lots of time so why not use it. For years I have hoped for a chance to get to the bottom of one of these hunt team classes. I would very much like to have the best six teams lined up. Then to have every horse jogged and I want them jogged, not cantered, until I am sure that they are traveling sound. Then I would like every horse cantered in a figure eight, and I'm going to do the best I can to discover whether they have mouths enough left so that a normal person can hold them when hounds are running, and if I can't decide it by looking at them I'm going to ride them. They can find me a saddle to put on the side-saddle horses, and I give fair warning that if I find a low, heavy-headed horse that bores and has no flex to his neck, my thumbs are down. I don't care what he looks like or how he jumped. The last few shows I have attended I have seen horses that a windlass would not hold win ladies' hunter classes. I saw a horse that was dead lame win a Corinthian class, and a broken-winded horse win a heavy-weight hunter class. We judges are driving the real horsemen out of the shows. If judges aren't willing or able to ride horses they shouldn't judge. If the show won't allot time to judge a class then judges should refuse to officiate."

"Well," said Henderson, "we'll be here all night and have every one in the place sore at us. They tell me the chestnut team has won this class for the last two years and I don't wonder. I never saw anything better."

Half an hour later Pat Dwyer and his lieutenants were retacking our horses. The judges were off by themselves apparently having a battle royal. It was during the resaddling operation that I learned to what perfection the Irish race has developed satire and irony, and comprehended afresh why every true Irishman must stand ever ready to do combat. I give it as my opinion that nothing short of combat can preserve self respect. Mr. Patrick Dwyer and Mr. Larry Sullivan, the Newcombes' man, were saddling their horses close by one another and I heard Mr. Sullivan say, "Mr. Dwyer, it's a holy shame the way one of your horses basted that third fince. I didn't see it or hear it, praise God, but they are all saying as how it sounded like a church struck by lightning, and I says to the boys, the pity on it, Mr. Dwyer couldn't have brought his horses over to me for one school afore the show. Sure and Mr. Newcombe would niver have minded being as he and Colonel Weatherford is sich friends; and Mr. Dwyer, it was sorry I was to hear the judge — the big one — say as how it was a grand pity that your horses had no bloom to 'em what with the grand style the gintlemen were got up in. The boys over at the gate was all saying as how you couldn't reach such big horses to clean 'em — but I says to the boys that whativer was the trouble I knew Mr. Dwyer had done his best and it's myself would tell Colonel Weatherford the same thing." I always thought that it was a happy coincidence that we mounted at that moment.

We were standing in front of the small pavilion used by the secretary, judges and stewards. The judges were some way off and still arguing. Suddenly they turned and came over to the pavilion and heard Duncan say to Mr. Dennison, the chairman, "Mr. Dennison, I'm very sorry but it seems impossible for Mr. Henderson and me to come to an accord, and we are going to ask you to select a third judge."

While we had been in the ring I had noticed H. Henry Hillison standing at the rail as an interested spectator. Apparently Dennison had also seen him, for he walked over and spoke with him and Hillison accompanied him into the ring. He shook hands with Duncan and Henderson and said, "I think I should make it clear that I have formed very definite opinions about this class from the side lines. I have been much interested in it. I never saw a class to equal it." Then Duncan said, "I don't feel like arguing about my selection. Why doesn't Hillison write his numbers on a card and if he agrees with either of us then we are through." Hillison had judged horses and hounds wherever horses and hounds had ever been exhibited in this country. He had ridden hunters and hunted hounds all his life and knew what constituted a hunt team, and unfortunately for the Colonel's team he had strong leanings towards blood horses. They handed him a card. He wrote four numbers on it, drew a circle around the numbers, wrote his initials at the bottom and handed the card back. Dennison examined the three cards and said, "The matter seems to have been solved, gentlemen. The committee is greatly obliged to you."

The teams were standing in the following order: Phyllis Newcombe's team was at the head, then a beautiful team of top middleweight brown horses, then our team, and a gray team back of us. All but six teams had been excused. The ring attendant who had been attaching the ribbons during the day took the judges' card from the secretary, gathered up four ribbons, put three of them and the card in his left hand, took the blue ribbon in his right and started to walk towards Phyllis Newcombe. I heard something which might have been a sigh or even a faint little gasp emanating from under a veil very close to me. Then Dennison came out of the pavilion carrying the trophy. He called the attendant to him, took the blue ribbon from him, glanced at the numbers on the card, and then he also started to walk towards Phyllis's team.

As he reached the three girls he took off his hat, and the girls showered him with smiles. Dennison asked them in whose name the team had been entered and Phyllis told him in her name. The old gentleman reached for her horse's head to attach the ribbon and said, "Your number is 14 isn't it?" "Why no," said Phyllis with a diminishing smile, "We are number 11." "Good gracious," said Mr. Dennison and called the attendant to him, put on his glasses, looked at the card, and started down the line. He looked at the number of the brown team and passed on; then he walked back of us and looked at our number and then I heard him saying, "Colonel Weatherford, who is the captain of this team?"—the Colonel answered, "This is Miss Sedgwick's team,"—saw Mr. Dennison affix the blue ribbon to the bridle of Mary's horse, saying, "Mary, I have presented this trophy many times, but never with so great pleasure as today." Mary tucked the trophy under her arm, we turned our horses' heads around, rode to and through the gate and the hunt team class of that year was over.

CHAPTER VII.

Colonel Weatherford's Brush

THE morning's mail brought me an invitation to dine at Colonel Weatherford's. It was one of those lugubrious things which start off — "Mr. John Weatherford requests" and so forth. Two or three times a year the Colonel girded up his loins and did this sort of thing. I don't think he enjoyed the functions but those who attended them did. If you were gastronomically minded you had a splendid time, and if you were of the younger generation you saw how your forebears were supposed to have dined and wined and were privileged to say to Smith the next day that you had toyed with some of old Weatherford's tawny port of '63 the night before.

As I started to accept the invitation I noticed that the dinner was being given on the Colonel's birthday. As he was never known to mention or refer to this day I thought it odd that he should commemorate it by a formal dinner. I had only learned of the date myself through a chance remark of one of his relatives.

When the evening of the dinner arrived we had hopped into our Indian summer and the weather was extremely close. It was with reluctance if not actual irritation that I encased myself in evening clothes. I would not have associated a dinner jacket with the state of the weather, but I am of that illogical majority who are persuaded that a dress coat is a smothering thing to wear.

When I arrived at the house the only car in sight was Enid Ashley's much used station wagon. I was then a few minutes late and I commented adversely upon the growing habit of people being late for dinner. After offering an ardent prayer that I might draw Enid at dinner I essayed the door. "They are in the library, Sir," the man said, and led the way. An odd place to receive, thought I. When I reached the library, a room which seemed as much mine as the Colonel's so much time did I spend in it, there was Enid Ashley, little Mary Sedgwick and Colonel Weatherford. The sight of Mary at such a supposedly old folks gathering surprised me. I had hardly more than shaken hands when the Colonel said, "Pendleton, if you will take Enid, and Mary will do me the honor, we will go in to dinner. This is our party. There is an old saying, 'the more the merrier, the fewer the better fare.' We are going to prove that it should run, 'the fewer the merrier, the more the better fare.' The fare may be frugal but I feel exceedingly merry."

The Colonel had said that he felt merry and he did. There is no cut and dried rule by which one can organize, promote or guarantee merriment. It slips quietly into the midst of all sorts of gatherings, at all sorts of places, and under all sorts of circumstances, causing people to expand and to think kindly of friends and neighbors and to go home convinced that this old world of ours is a grand place in which to have one's being.

We four had much in common. Each had a good horse and at least three of us knew one when we saw it, and I was learning. We thoroughly enjoyed foxhunting and were keenly in-

terested in our hounds and what they did. We could have sat
together hour after hour following a good run and argued
and expounded the doings of the fox and the pack. Foxhunting is a great leveler of ages. No one was young and no one
was old. We were just four enthusiastic foxhunters.

When we were back in the library after dinner, Mary, who
was sitting on the couch between Enid and me, got up, walked
over to the back of the Colonel's chair, put her hands on his
shoulders and said, "Colonel Weatherford, Mr. Pendleton
whispered to me that this is your birthday. I'm awfully sorry
I didn't know about it. I guess it's too late for me to do anything now, but I have a wonderful idea. You know, they say
it's better to give than to receive. Would you promise to give
me something if I wanted it very much?" The conservatism
of a lifetime slipped from the Colonel or was it that he knew
the child so well. He hit his knee a fine round whack and
vowed that Mary should have anything she wanted.

Mary looked up over the fireplace and said, "Colonel
Weatherford I want the story of your brush more than anything I can think of. I have never seen the brush before but I
often hear people talk about it. Will you tell it to us? Please
do. I know Mrs. Ashley wants to hear it. She told me so.
We've had such a wonderful time and if we could only hear
how you got the brush, your birthday party would be perfect;
and please Colonel Weatherford, couldn't we come here just
like this every year on your birthday — just we four?"

When we in our hunting country wished to convey the
thought that a thing would probably not come to pass, we were
wont to say, "Oh, it will happen when Colonel Weatherford
tells how he won his brush."

This saying had even filtered down into the vocabulary of

small children, for I heard my nephew, aged eleven, say to his sister, "I do wish Dad would let me hunt *Old Piedmont,* but I don't suppose he ever will until Colonel Weatherford tells how he won his brush."

The brush in question hung in a specially constructed niche over the library fireplace, where in Italy or Spain one would have expected to see a small polychromed figure of a Saint.

Weatherford never gave the impression of being the least secretive regarding the trophy, but rather waved the subject aside as being of no moment, or too long a story to tell. Yet one could not help feeling that a man who had hunted all his life, and went as well as he did, would never display a solitary brush in such a conspicuous manner unless it had a worthy history.

If this matter had assumed undue importance, I think it was because a number of women had from time to time made trifling wagers that they would pry the story loose.

There was an uncomfortably long silence, then the Colonel said, "Mary, the only objection I have felt about telling the story is that I'm just a bit sentimental about the little affair, and one is sometimes reluctant to air such things. I will, however, gladly tell you about it if you wish, and if you will all bear with me in the telling."

THE STORY OF THE BRUSH

She was a bewitching little English girl of twelve whose lot had been temporarily cast in these alien United States through the business activities of her father, a dominant figure in the world of shipping.

At the hoary age of two and fifty I had fallen head-over-heels in love with her and found myself playing the rôles of sporting companion, admirer, and father confessor. It is hard to recall, and harder to explain, how such affairs have their beginnings. I presume the child supplied a want the very existence of which was unknown to me until she so winsomely crept into my heart.

Horses had become her all absorbing passion, and that which should have been but a minor interest had become a too engrossing theme. We all recognized this, but only when it was too late, and I who had so fervently aided and abetted it had somewhat to regret. That she was more intense than other children we knew, but where was the yardstick with which one might measure such intensity?

For two years she and I had revelled in a rollicking welter of horse lore. We read all manner of books on horses and hunting. We recited verses, sang songs and pored over pictures featuring the horse.

On my visits to her parents she would resort to all the feminine subterfuges of the ages to get me alone, and then in that serious, quizzical way of hers would press her search. What did the book you brought me last week mean when it said so and so? Why did it say that a huntsman should never do this or that? She toiled through Beckford, devoured Lord Willoughby deBroke, and caused my copy of Henry Higginson's *The Hunts of the United States and Canada*, to look like a nursery copy of the *Water Babies*. Whyte-Melville's *Riding Recollections* she could quote ad lib. Even the ancient spelling and letters of my first edition of Somerville's great poem could not discourage her.

It would have been her greatest joy to have squeezed in

between Dick Christian and The Druid when they took their famous trip in the gig through Leicestershire, preparing Dick's lecture. It might or might not have pleased Harry Worcester Smith and Harry Page to have known that she considered them to be of the same era as John Mytton and Captain John White. A picture of Mr. Smith on *The Cad* was one of her treasures but she seemed intolerant of the idea that both horse and rider were not of the later eighteenth century. I once pointed out Henry Vaughan to her, whom she knew to be a real, live, present-day M.F.H. She fairly glued her eyes on his spectacular height, accentuated by his gray top hat, and said she wished she lived next door to Mr. Vaughan so she could see him start off every single morning in his pink coat and on Sundays with his grey hat.

With a child's love of the superlative she used to ask, "Who do you suppose was the greatest rider in all the world? I mean ever and ever? Who do you guess was the greatest huntsman that ever was known in the very whole world? Don't you think that there must have been some horse some time that was just ever so much the greatest hunter in the world? Don't you know which one it was, Colonel John? You have read all of the books. Don't you know? Do you think it might have been some horse of Squire Osbaldeston's or Mr. Assheton Smith's, or maybe Mr. Whyte-Melville's? Somebody just must have had the greatest hunter."

I once asked her why she wanted so much to know, and she told me it was because when she went to bed she would close her eyes and play a game of pretending, and would pretend that she was hunting with the great Will Long, who must always be on his white mare, *Bertha,* just as they looked in the picture in her room. And there would be Squire Osbaldeston, Assheton Smith, Dick Christian, Mr. Meynell, Whyte-Melville. She said the only thing she had to ride was Squire Osbaldeston's *Slasher*, and that surely in all the world I must know of a greater horse than *Slasher*, and that it would spoil her pretending if she did not know that she was on the greatest horse of all time. I felt like telling her that each and every one of my friends — men and women — particularly the latter, would confess to being the owner of the dream-horse needed for her pretending.

I had carried her off to witness all sorts of sporting events. I had held a feverish little hand at international polo matches, and the running of the Brook Steeplechase. We had run ourselves breathless to keep horses in view at amateur race meets, and burst into convulsive sobs when a horse was killed. We had junketed to the Genesee Valley and Virginia in search of an ideal horse for her and were pleased to think we had found it, — and carefully planned to see the Maryland Cup en route.

All these things were wondrous good fun, yet deep down in our hearts we knew that they were but the forerunners of our one high and all absorbing ambition, our first foxhunt. What hours and hours we had spent discussing this project! I longed to take her hunting as I have longed for few things before or since, yet I rather dreaded the event. The responsibility gave me concern, as she seemed too young for the pitfalls of the hunting field; yet I think I feared more the risk of disappointment to her. She was fairly steeped in the traditions of the shires of England. Her mind was aglow with the rich panoply of the hunt with all its color, action and thrills, and I flunked at the risk of disillusionment. However, I well knew that the day could not be indefinitely postponed.

At the time of which I tell I was maintaining a small week-end establishment in one of the older hunting countries, to which I would motor over the week-ends and on such other hunting days as I could get away. A flare-up in my menage had temporarily discommoded me, and pending the procuring of new servants I had closed the cottage.

On a Friday, toward the end of October, I dropped in for luncheon with Maida Elizabeth's parents, en route to the country where I had planned to spend the night with the M.F.H., hunt in the morning and perhaps stay on for a few days. We dawdled through luncheon, and just as I was preparing to leave I felt a soft little arm steal around my neck, and what to me were the most adorable brown curls in the world tickling my ear, the whole resulting and terminating in my being kissed. Maida Elizabeth had returned from school. Was I going to hunt on the morrow? When, Colonel John, could she come hunting? Why hadn't I been in to see her for ever so long? Had I kept my hunting diary after every single run this autumn as I had promised, and please wouldn't I bring it to her the very next time?

"Maida Elizabeth," I said, "if I had any one in that cottage of mine to take care of us and cook for us, I would take you up with me this very day if your mother and father would let you go. Indeed I would."

She lapsed into silence while I talked with her parents. I can see her so plainly, even now, sitting on a low stool, leaning forward, and apparently reviewing some weighty matter. A half century of bachelorhood may suggest some discrimination in the matter of the feminine eye, and I say in all seriousness that neither before nor since have I seen such expressive, questioning, searching eyes. She was wont to look down when thinking, then raise a pair of very telling eyelashes and look straight at and into you. A Russian painter who made an impress through his work on this country, told me that he thought the child had one of the most beautiful faces he had ever seen and with great tenacity badgered her mother without avail to permit Maida Elizabeth to sit for him as a model.

When the general conversation lapsed she came over, sat down beside me and snuggling her hand into mine as she did on rare occasions, said, "Colonel John, I can cook a little; I could wash and put away the dishes, and I learned all about making beds when I went to camp. Don't you think if I worked and tried as hard as anything I could take care of just you and me, just for one day — just for one day. Colonel John? Don't you think maybe I could?"

That was too much. In thirty minutes I had her in the car, bag and baggage, and as Scott said of Marjorie Fleming when he carried her off on winter nights, "We'll hep'it up."

Perched on the back seat, and also off for their first hunt, were a pair of diminutive black boots with brass plates on the trees proclaiming them to be the property of Maida Elizabeth Barminster. An indulgent father had failed to realize that $110 boots and hollow trees that fit at twelve years may not fit at fourteen.

We motored a long time in silence. She was never wont to chatter. Knowing her so well I understood that her feelings were very tense, and that no one could possibly appreciate how momentous an event this seemed to her.

Of our adventures at light housekeeping I will say little. I retain a happy picture and remembrance of it. I recall entering my bedroom hours after she had gone to the land of nod and finding the bed neatly turned down, a pair of companionable old red slippers poking their worn toes out from under the bed, and on the night table a vase of fall asters.

She ate practically no dinner, saying she felt all tight and funny inside. I knew the symptoms. I too had felt "sort of sicky and funny inside," just before riding my first race years ago.

We awoke to as perfect a hunting day as this well-favored land of ours can produce.

While dressing and contemplating the problems incident to preparing palatably a breakfast which would tide us over until our return at perhaps four or five o'clock, I heard a decidedly authoritative bustling going on in the kitchen.

Mrs. Tim Templer, bless her heart, had come over from the Kennels to get breakfast for us.

She had heard in that mysterious way in which country people hear so much that we were "in residence" and, as she said, "like enough to be helpless."

Tim told me that he had won Mrs. Tim away from a belted Earl. After that breakfast I was surprised that the Magna Charta, The Bill of Rights, or even the Writ of Habeas Corpus, had saved Tim after stealing such a cook from an Earl.

I was perplexed at first as to which of my horses would best carry Maida Elizabeth, but fixed upon a fourteen-year-old clean bred horse called *Lord Autumn*, doing his ninth season. He was a safe, capable, courageous horse but inclined to be a trifle domineering.

At the Meet I was punctilious in introducing Maida Elizabeth to the Master and the more gallant of our first flighters. I knew she would place much stress on this formality.

A good many years have rolled by since that morning, but I remember feeling inordinately proud of her. It was odd that so retiring and silent a child should invariably make such an impression upon people. She had an exquisite immaculateness in putting herself together, difficult to describe and impossible to emulate.

We moved off and drew a nearby covert but with no success. Then for two hours we drifted mile upon mile across a red and golden landscape, drawing as we went. Many of the field dropped out in favor of bridge and tea. Others as usual grumbled at the lack of foxes and talked of other days, but hounds drew on.

From time to time I would ride up to Maida Elizabeth just for the pleasure of watching her. She seemed absorbed and disinclined to talk. Only once she spoke, "Colonel John, isn't it more glorious than anything else in the whole world?" and smiled in a way which suggested that we alone of all the field, yes of all the fields of the world, knew the joys of fox hunting.

The hoped for "two o'clock fox" failed us.

At three o'clock we were drawing an important covert from which if a fox were found and bustled out we were reasonably sure of some sort of a run. The field had dwindled to not above a dozen.

Of a sudden a hound opened at the far end of the covert. I recognized it to be *Big Echo*, a hound I had walked for the Hunt, and so named by reason of a loud and resounding voice, and I knew from many talks with old Tim Templer, the huntsman, that this hound never opened unless sure he was right. I also knew that Tim, from somewhere in the labyrinth of the covert, was cocking his ear and making it his business to move up nearer to the hound.

Drawing a little to one side I signaled to Maida Elizabeth

to come with me. I then very casually and in as offhand manner as possible, edged down towards the woods. The rest of the field continued "coffee-housing" but then they were all old stagers and did not have a Maida Elizabeth to save from the disappointment of a blank day or losing a run.

Again the deep voice of *Big Echo* resounded and a second later a hound with a thin, choppy, impatient voice honored.

The covert was on my right. The M.F.H. was some way on in front, talking to an apparently agitated farmer. I noticed him turn, look towards the covert as the hound spoke, and knew he was casting about for a method of terminating his conversation. I felt apprehensive about being so far from the center of action at this particular covert, so, at the risk of teaching my little charge bad hunting manners, and having a bad five minutes myself with the Master, I decided to slip into the covert and be prepared to go out on the far side in good company with hounds should they break that way. I was determined on this day of all days to get well away if I could possibly manage it.

We had not ridden above a few hundred yards in covert when hounds opened with a great resounding burst of music and seemed fairly to crash out of the far side. As I looked up I saw old Tim directly ahead of us on his redoubtable grey horse, *Suds*. A hard pair of old timers, those two.

Maida Elizabeth snuggled into Tim's "pocket," and we scurried through a long wood ride towards the open country. Looking ahead I saw a break in the tree tops indicating cleared land, and just in front a formidable barway of new, black, whippy saplings dividing the covert from the open pastures.

Tim was setting a terrific pace, and in no very good humor, having been delayed in covert through bustling up a dead end wood ride which took him nowhere. He was now bent on getting on good terms with his hounds.

Tim was a better huntsman than he was a rider, particularly in moments of high stress. He approached the barway with his horse extended and not a leg under him with which to jump. *Suds* hit the barway to an extent which caused the saplings, as is ever the way of saplings, to bend and rattle but not break. The grey horse, to whom this experience was no novelty, pecked on to his nose, scraped and bumped along the rocky wood ride for some distance, now on his knees, then on his chin, encouraged to do his best or worst by Tim's dictatorial voice and virile language. Tim's legs were dangling about in a seemingly futile effort to synthesize them with his fluttering stirrup irons.

Maida Elizabeth pulled *Lord Autumn* down to a walk to give Tim and *Suds* room in which to complete their evolutions. When they were out of the way she took the old horse by the head, him who they all said had no mouth, and brought him into the barway beautifully collected. They made a perfect jump and were gone. I scrambled over after them.

We were now crossing a grand bit of turf, with hounds well on and carrying a good head. For myself I was none too well fixed for a big run. I was riding a spectacular looking five-year-old that had sold for a King's ransom at Saratoga as a yearling. A knowledgeable trainer had discarded him as a racing prospect and I was trying to make a hunter of him. He was a delightful ride for as long as he lasted, but seemed to have little interest in the sport.

We raced along over Twyford Bottom with Mellick's Woods two miles ahead and to the west. I rather thought the fox might den in those woods and that we should call it a day.

Instead of that the line scouted the woods for its entire length and then veered northeast towards Steptoe Hill. This was two miles as the fox ran, but we, to avoid Mulgrave Swamp, had to tack on an extra mile and at a pace which boded no good for me.

I heard horses behind me and saw the M.F.H. and five of the hard riding brigade pounding after us pretty much wide open, as though they expected the thing to be over any minute. Little did they guess what they were in for.

By the time we had reached the stone-strewn sheep pasture that lies at the foot of Steptoe, the Master and Maida Elizabeth were both in Tim's "pocket," while I was laboring in the rear with a rapidly tiring young horse under me.

There is a famous earth in a rocky ledge in that sheep pasture. I knew the spot well. Surely, I thought, he will go to earth there. Standing up in my stirrups I located the rocks, but even as I looked hounds passed them by and were a hundred yards beyond. They were running beautifully packed with great drive and heading north. I could see the white steeple of Smithborough Church far ahead.

We had entered a cattle country where farmers insisted on stout enclosures, and the fences took a bit of real doing. I was perceptibly dropping to the rear. The hard riding brigade had been reduced to three, but those were well up and in front of me. If ever I detested a horse it was that magnificent looking, 16.2 hand chestnut thoroughbred. He had hit the last three fences fore and aft. He was now proceeding on the theory that it was entirely my duty and responsibility to hold his head up for him and was leaning on the bit accordingly.

I could still see old Tim pounding along on his white horse with Maida Elizabeth and the Master in his wake. Of a sudden an urge came over me to be up front and share the child's feelings. I wanted so much to see her in a rôle we had often pictured in our talks. If I were ever to make it I must act promptly, for I was fast getting to the bottom of my horse.

I judge it to have been a long time since any one had been rough with that colt. His good looks and amiable disposition had insured him an easy life; but now he had an interesting experience for about five minutes. I rode him with determination and a disregard of consequences. He hit a stiff, upstanding post-and-rail fence so hard that he twisted and corkscrewed until I had nothing between me and the ground, but he managed to disentangle one foot in time to use it as a prop and so stood up.

I at last drew up with *Lord Autumn* and my reward was worth many times the effort. I wish a master might have produced a picture for me of Maida Elizabeth as I saw her at that moment. I think I had counted on seeing a hot, wide-eyed, disheveled little child. Instead I looked upon a face that was just as I had seen it when I first beckoned her to follow me. Her great eyes were looking far ahead towards the hounds. Her exquisite chin was tilted up as though trying to make herself taller and so see farther. She was sitting as nonchalantly as in an armchair. Such composure and ease I think I never saw on a galloping horse. The usually domineering and self-willed *Lord Autumn* was striding along with hardly a touch on the reins. The horse had never performed so since he was foaled. I was conscious of experiencing a tinge of uneasiness as I looked at her. People didn't cross difficult countries in terrific runs on strange horses or on any other horse that way. The Master, a two-fisted and essentially practical person of no imagination, didn't like it either, and when I asked him long afterwards what he didn't like, he was unable to tell me, but said he felt as though he had Joan of Arc beside him for all those miles, and would never again speak of it, which perplexed me.

Hearing me come alongside, she turned, and again her look was suggestive of a great and glorious secret between us; but neither of us spoke. We galloped side by side for a few fields, then I again dropped back. The colt had shot his bolt.

We had left the hamlet of Smithborough on our right, and hounds were still running hard, with the line bending to the northeast. About three miles on was as far as our hounds had ever hunted to the north. Then *terra incognita.*

There was one thing I could do which might at least keep me in distant touch with the run. It was a meagre chance but better than giving up.

On my left was a high, wooded ridge extending well to the north but not more than half a mile in width. Should the fox continue north and round the point of the ridge, he might then head south or east, permitting me to nick in again.

I took a clumsy fall in reaching a grassy lane to which I could find no barway or gate. Picking myself up, I jogged down the lane towards the ridge. Before entering the woods I climbed a knoll to have one final look at the disappearing field. At the far end of an extensive meadow I saw the Master on the ground and the last of the hard-riding brigade standing with him. Whatever had happened, they were both now out of the run. This put another aspect on the matter. As long as the Master had kept going I felt reasonably comfortable about Maida Elizabeth, but now she was following the most devil-may-care rider in seven states over a difficult country, and approaching a region unknown to any of us. She was undoubtedly riding a tired horse. I was in a blue funk.

There appearing nothing that I could do better than what I was doing, I pressed on through and over the ridge hoping against hope.

The wood ride was longer and rougher than I had expected. When I finally emerged into the open and pulled up, I was standing at the top of a long rise from where I could view the country to the north, south and east.

A fine October day was rapidly drawing to a close, and as I stood there nothing broke the stillness but the faint chirping of a bird in the bushes back of me, and the far away lowing of a cow complaining of a tardy farmer.

I scanned the horizon for any moving object and strained my ears in listening, but it was evident that no hounds were running on that side of the ridge.

Surely there is no lonesomeness met with in any of our games or sports like unto that which creeps over him who in the hour of twilight seeks alone for hounds on the line of the hunted fox.

I took out my pipe and as I lifted my head from lighting it, I was looking towards the north. Far in the distance something was moving across a field. I finally made it out to be cattle. Perchance hounds had disturbed them. I kept looking until my eye caught also a rapidly moving white horse and something following close behind. Hounds were plainly still running hard and heading somewhat north.

Below in the valley a dusty country road meandered into the North Country and I determined to take it and plug on. I cajoled the disheartened son of a St. Leger winner into a toe-stubbing jog and essayed the endless looking road.

I had progressed in this fashion for some way when a boy passed me in a car and directly ahead turned into a farmyard. I called to him, asked if I might put my tired horse in his stable and would he, for a consideration, take me a few miles north to search for a little girl for whom I was looking. He agreed and we chugged north. We presently passed the field in which I had seen the cattle moving. They were now complacently huddled together in one corner. From that point we stopped the car every quarter of a mile to listen. As daylight slipped into twilight we came to a gate marking the end of the road through which we passed. From this point the land rose to great stretches of bare hills used only as sheep pastures. It seemed an endless country and very sombre.

The boy said we could run the car most any place on the "barrens" as he called them, so, where did I want to go? I told him to take me to a broad plateau to the north. Upon reaching this I left the car that I might the better listen. The Ford was gurgling, bubbling and panting so plaintively that one could not have heard hounds running fifty yards away. When well clear of the car I listened, and there, far on before me was Tim's horn calling hounds to him. I suppose I have had, I must have had, more stirring thrills than that mellow horn gave me as it floated across the lonely drear hillside in the fading October light, but the memory of no other thrill is quite so clear and persistent.

I sprinted to the car as I had never thought to sprint in top boots and we essayed the alarmingly steep ascent from the plateau to the uppermost reaches of the barrens.

Then we came upon them, a weather-beaten old man in a scarlet coat, and standing beside him with its head between its knees was a very distressed white horse. A few yards away a wee mite of a child was holding a fox's brush with the end tied up in a large, soiled cotton handkerchief. She wore a velvet cap far back on her head, and across her beautiful forehead was a splash of crimson. Tim had blooded her. The hounds were stretched out in the attitudes tired hounds assume.

Off by herself and uttering low yet spiteless growls was a lemon-and-white bitch, *Magic*, with the mask in her mouth. It was her mask for it had been her fox. When *Big Echo* opened she had been the first to honor him. Blessed with a magnificent nose and great foot, she had been first out of cover and had stuck relentlessly to the line all through the lengthening hours of that golden afternoon. When her unfathomable instinct told her that the fox — her fox — was sinking, she mustered all her remaining energy, scaled the last ascent and killed him on the crest. It was to Tim Templer's honor that he would ever see justice done, and so *Magic* was alone with her mask.

When I came up Tim looked at me, jerked his finger to his forehead as was his wont, but neither smiled nor spoke. *Lord Autumn* was standing off by himself with the reins tied to a sapling and his girths loosened. He was looking far down the hillside to where some sheep were moving. I put my arm through his reins and led him over and sat down beside Maida Elizabeth. I filled my pipe and when I had it well going she put her arm in mine. I don't know how long we may have sat, nor do I remember that we said anything. From time to time I heard Tim blow his horn, but it seemed far off. I know my pipe burned itself out.

Then Tim moved on leading *Lord Autumn* beside him and the weary hounds in his wake.

[123]

It was dark when Tim reached the farm, where I had requisitioned the car and there he stayed the night for the horses could travel no further.

A tired little girl whose fingers twitched every now and then, snuggled down beside me in the car, and slipped her hand into mine. Every so often a sigh would find its way up from the depths of a red blanket loaned us by a friendly but perplexed farmer's wife.

I suppose the turning-in to my driveway was as the slow falling of a curtain at the end of a play. It distinctly marked the end of our first hunt. As we approached the house, I heard: "Oh, Colonel John, it was wonderful. So wonderful I can't talk about it. I never want to talk of it to anybody — not even you. Please, Colonel John, don't let anybody talk to me about it. I want it all for my very own. Perhaps I won't ever want to see Tim or *Suds* again. I want them to be for ever and ever just as they were for all those miles and up that last great hill with the fox in front, and the hounds hardly able to catch him. That was where Tim couldn't go any further and he took off his cap and made me put it on and gave me his horn and said, 'Take 'em, Missie — I never had to do it afore, but take 'em, Missie, and God help you catch him.' That's what he said, and *Lord Autumn* and I went to the top of the hill, and they killed the fox, but I didn't know what to do, and my mouth was all dry and stuck together, and I couldn't make any sound. Then Tim came up and everything."

She said she couldn't even think of *Lord Autumn* without feeling cryey.

When I reached the cottage I tucked her in bed, brought her a light supper, and put a bell on the table so that she could

" . . . and they killed the fox."

ring for me. When I said good night and stooped to take a last look at those searching eyes which always intrigued me, she seemed fain to let me go.

Fearful that the strain might have been too much for her, I lamented that I had not insisted on her pulling out. Then I thought, "who was I to talk of telling her to pull out who could not even keep her coat tails in view?"

The next morning Mrs. Tim came over, prepared breakfast, and put things in order. As we sat on the lounge together after breakfast, Maida Elizabeth said she wished she could live for ever and ever just with me, and never grow up, and hunt with Tim and me, and that of all things in the whole world she hated birthdays the most, and wished time would stand still so that Tim and *Suds* and *Lord Autumn* and I would not change, and that now she had Tim for her pretend huntsman instead of Will Goodall, and *Lord Autumn* in place of *Slasher*, and was never going to pretend about any one except them and me. Then she was whisked away home in the car.

I moved over to stay with the M.F.H., and the weather remaining fine and the sport good, stayed on about ten days.

Upon reaching home I found a letter from Maida Elizabeth's father written on shipboard telling me that he had been quite suddenly recalled to England, where he hoped I would soon visit them, and thanking me for taking Maida Elizabeth hunting. He was sure she must have had a good time, but she had not been very exhaustive in her description of the visit; that once when her mother had pressed her for an account of the hunt, Maida had burst into tears and left the room, from which they were afraid she had perhaps not conducted herself properly, or had ridden badly.

Each Christmas brought me a card from the family and an

invitation to visit them. In October of each year, mailed so as to reach me as near as possible to a certain day, I would receive a letter from Maida Elizabeth. They were long letters telling me the events of her year, but there was never even a veiled reference to our great run or to Tim, or in fact anything connected with our hunt. She was true to her word. She had locked it all in her heart.

Six years rolled away. One fair May morning I received in the mail an envelope addressed in her father's handwriting. It flashed through my mind that it might be an announcement of his intended return to America. A feeling of expectancy stole over me, unlocking countless memories dear to my heart. I found myself projecting all sorts of new adventures with Maida Elizabeth. As a result I felt reluctant to open the letter fearful of disappointment. On the film of the past which was unreeling itself across my memory, was that moment after the greatest run in the history of our hounds, when I had leaned down to kiss her good night, and she in her weariness and tenseness had seemed loath to have me leave her. I knew it to have been the only time in my life that any one had felt this way about me. I finally determined to run over to England during the summer, and as soon as I had decided upon this, I felt reconciled to opening the envelope. It contained a clipping from an English paper.

"On May the first at Higher St. Albans, Dorset, Maida Elizabeth, aged eighteen, the only child of Sir Francis Barminster, Bart., and Lady Barminster."

The obituary told nothing more.

I sat I know not how long, now and again looking up at a photo on my mantel. Then I ordered my horse tacked, and went for a ride.

As I passed the kennels I saw old Tim astride of *Suds*. He was riding back and forth in the far corner of the meadow with his puppies, while two boys followed on foot.

I wanted to talk with some one, so I rode into the meadow and said, "Tim, do you remember the little girl who was with you when you killed the fox that day on the North Barrens?" And Tim said, "Colonel, I've forgot the half of all the ladies and gentlemen who ever hunted with these hounds, but the wee missie is more with me, so help me God, than even my old woman. It's never into the North Country I get that I don't think on her. I'm an old man getting to be, Sir. It's forty-eight years I've ridden to hounds, and over thirty I've hunted 'em, and there was never the like of the thing that happened to any huntsman in the old country or this, as when I couldn't go on and gave me cap and horn to that bairn on the sheep hills in the dark and bade her go on to a kill. I knowed I shoulda stopped hounds, Sir — I knowed it, Sir, or leastaways tried to stop 'em — and Colonel, I did blow once, but then she put her hand on my arm and looked at me like I was never looked at afore. Colonel, people like me don't ever have people with them kind of eyes look at 'em that way, and she said, 'Please, Tim, I want just ever so much to go on to the very end. Please, please, don't blow.' Those were her very words. It was then I give her me old cap and horn."

"Tim," I said, "the little girl died a week ago in England." And then wished I had never told him.

People like Tim don't do or say anything when they are hurt. "Thank you, Sir," was all he said, and turned back to his puppies.

I rode on in a listless manner for about an hour, then returned to the house and wrote a letter to England.

During each spring season, and upon a day just to my liking, I would go off on an all day riding picnic. This annual event had become a rite which I looked forward to. I had fixed upon the following Sunday for the outing, providing the day proved auspicious.

The weather favoring me on that morning I was up, mounted, and on the road in good season. On these occasions I rode in a well-worn British army saddle, the pouches of which were filled, even including a nip of Amontillado sherry, which the label informed me had been shipped by Mackenzie's Co., Ferez de la Frontera, Spain.

On these rides I would always reach the outer fringe of the hunting country, and very often some miles beyond. I started towards the north and being mounted on a particularly free moving horse, tucked a good many miles behind me by early noon.

I was picking my way over a rocky section of what seemed more like a farm lane than a road, when upon looking up I saw a group of farm buildings, which had a familiar look and I recognized the farm at which Maida Elizabeth, Tim and I had put up our horses. I determined to press on to the hill country, and if possible find the spot where the fox had been killed on that memorable day.

I finally reached the gate marking the end of the lane, let myself through and essayed the long ascent that must have brought old *Suds* to a standstill. I was tugging on up and marveling at the power and endurance of horses and hounds that makes it possible for them to gallop over half a county and at the end face such a hill. I had crossed the plateau from which I had heard Tim's horn and was close to the summit when to my amazement I saw Tim. He was dismounted, with *Suds* standing near by, and evidently engrossed in some activity. My first impulse was to hail him, but on second thought I decided not to. As both Tim and *Suds* had their backs to me, I turned and rode down until I was completely out of sight. There was a meagre plantation of stunted trees and bushes off to my left. I rode back of these, determined to wait until Tim had completed whatever he was doing and had departed. It did not seem as though I wanted to talk to him just then, yet having come so far I wanted to stand alone on the very spot where I had come upon Maida Elizabeth with her brush and Tim's cap and the daub of blood on her forehead.

I had waited perhaps a quarter of an hour, when, peeking through the bushes, I saw Tim riding slowly down. *Suds* had grown very white. In this off season his mane and tail had been allowed to grow. He looked hollow-backed and old, and I thought rather pathetic.

Tim was dressed in disreputable old clothes. The whole picture was rather of a weary farmer plodding his solitary course astride an ancient work horse.

When I thought the way was clear, I took the course Tim had come down. As I reached the summit, I saw ahead of me and slightly to the left, a mound of rough field stones some three feet high. From the center of the mound extended a length of chestnut fence-rail, silvery gray in color, to which a board had been crudely nailed.

I dismounted and walked over to the mound. On the board scrawled in large, ill-formed letters, I read:

THIS IS WHERE HER AND ME
KILLED THAT FOX

I followed Tim down the hill.

Towards the end of the following week a package arrived for me. Upon opening it I found a card reading, "These remembrances are forwarded pursuant to the last wish of Maida Elizabeth Barminster."

I sat alone on my terrace through the slowly waning twilight of a June evening, with a fox's brush in my hand and a child's little hunting crop on the seat beside me marked for Tim.

CHAPTER VIII.

The East Oil City Hunt and Social Club

ONE December morning Colonel Weatherford and I
stopped at the village post office to pick up our mail en route
to town where we were to catch the Congressional for Washington and go on to Middleburg, Virginia, for two weeks'
hunting. We lapsed into silence in our respective corners of
his commodious Lancaster car, an ancient, ponderous conveyance, and perused our letters and newspapers. In the Colonel's
mail was a package of proof sheets of an article he was writing on some phase of archaeology, which he glanced over
hurriedly while I delved into a book catalogue from the
Anderson Galleries.

Suddenly from the Colonel's side of the car I heard "God
bless my soul," and glanced over at him. He had put his
proof sheets away and was reading a voluminous looking
letter. A minute or two later I heard, "Bless my soul! what
an extraordinary person." In the many years I had known
the old gentleman I had seldom heard him express surprise
or astonishment at anything he heard or saw, but his face now
had the look I would have expected to see on it had some one
invited him to lunch at a downtown restaurant.

I went back to my catalogue but was conscious from time
to time of the Colonel straightening himself up, crinkling the
papers, taking off his glasses, then putting them back on again

with a jerk, and staring fiercely at the letters. It seemed to me his long gray mustache had a bellicose air about it.

Finally he turned and, glaring at me as though I might have been the unfortunate author of whatever he had been reading, said, "Pendleton, did you ever read a book called *The Unbearable Bassington* by a chap named Munroe — an inimical book?" "No," I said, "I have never read it." "Well," he said, "Munroe suggests that religion has become unpopular due to its having become too generally adopted, and I assure you, Pendleton, foxhunting is coming to the same pass. Here, read this. I have just received it from Henry Maughn."

I read the following correspondence:

Dear Colonel Weatherford:

I enclose herewith copy of the application of the East Oil City Hunt and Social Club seeking recognition by this Association.

The matter will come up for consideration at the next meeting of the Executive Committee which I trust you will find it possible to attend.

I have not included the history to which the letter refers as it is somewhat voluminous, but will have it at the Meeting, where it will be available to the Members of the Committee.

Faithfully,

HENRY MAUGHN,
Secretary.

I read on.

Mr. Henry Maughn,
Sec. Master of American Fox Dogs,
Boston, Mass.

Dear Friend:

I take pen in hand to write you as one hunter and Master of Fox Dogs to another about our East Oil City Hunt and Social Club. As you can see from my name being printed at the top of this letter I am Master of our hunt dogs.

Now Mr. Maughn what I want to be wised up on is this. We want to be known as a recognitioned pack. What do we have to do to get this way.

Our Club takes a Magazine called *Saddle and Bridle*. It's a dandy mag. You ought to take it. Every once in a while it tells you how to dress to go hunting and those sort of things. Well Friend Maughn we read it pretty careful and we see it carries a long list of hunts which have been recognitioned so we want to be. Please send me all the works just as soon as you can do it. I would sure like to see you out here some time. Maybe when we are recognitioned you would have to come out here as Sec and look us over. We sure will give you a good time. Well this will be all for now.

Yours truly,

OTTO SCHMALTZ,
M.F.H.

Otto Schmaltz, Esq., M.F.H.,
East Oil City Hunt and Social Club,
East Oil City.

Dear Sir:

I have for acknowledgement your esteemed favor of November 20th relative to the recognition of your hounds.

As a condition precedent to the consideration of an application for the recognition of your hunt by this Association it is essential that the Association be apprised of certain matters.

Upon receipt of the following information your application will be presented to the Executive Committee for consideration and action:

(1) Brief history of your organization.
(2) Length of time you have hunted the country.
(3) Quarry hunted.
(4) Breed of hounds — English, American, Cross-bred.
(5) Character of your country.
(6) Location and extent of country. (Kindly include a map with boundaries indicated in red).
(7) Number of couples in kennels.
(8) Character of obstacles met with.
(9) Disposition of land owners.
(10) Duration of season.
(11) Name of huntsman.
(12) Nearest R.R. Station — telegrams, mail and express.

Yours truly,

HENRY MAUGHN,
Secretary.

Henry Maughn,
Sec. Masters of American Fox Dogs,
Boston, Mass.

Dear Friend:

I received your letter a week ago last Friday. Now I don't want you to think I wouldn't have answered it sooner if I

could, but I've been working on the thing ever since I got it
besides being busy in the store.

First about the history part. After I got your letter we held
a meeting and made a resolution in bang up shape so as our
sec would write a history of our club showing you the whole
works. I have pinned it to the last page of this letter. Our sec
is Miss Eliza Sweetapple who is the librarian over to our
library. She sure did a swell job. Read what she says about
me. You can keep this copy to show the other M.F.H's., for
we have another one.

Next you wanted to know how long we have hunted the
country. Eliza says this must be a mistake on your girl's part
because she says you can't hunt a country and must mean how
long we have followed our dogs. Of course we have followed
them and had chases ever since our club was started which is
a year ago but if you mean how long have people hunted out
here in these parts, why Friend Maughn I don't know. I
asked old man Peake who says he is eighty-six and has a good
rabbit dog, and he says his father kept a couple of dogs before him. I should think Mr. Maughn that that would make
us a pretty old hunting country.

Next you ask what quarry we hunt. Well this is sure a
stickler for us folks. This is mostly a flat country. I don't
guess there is any quarrying done this side of Brillsburgh and
that's close to three hundred and fifty miles. I suppose if we
had to do it to get our dogs recognitioned we could ship some
of them up to Brillsburgh and run 'em in a quarry if we
could find one, and make a deal with the owners. Please write
me full particulars of how you do it. I guess it's some new
trick for making them handy and the like of that.

Next is the breed of dogs — English, American, Cross-

[135]

breed. I don't guess any of 'em were ever to England — May be not even out of Dike County. About them being a cross breed I don't call any of 'em cross except it might be "Sarah" that we got from a colored farmer over at Hainsville, and she's not what you'd call right cross, but there is no use of me holding anything back and "Sarah" did bite that English huntsman what Eliza's history shows we had so much trouble with, but we could get rid of her easy enough.

Now about the character of our country. It's good. There hasn't been a lynching here since 1893 and that's before I had anything to do with the place, and no one from around here has ever been electrocuted up at State Prison since ever the place was built. You don't have to give this a thought. I got Judge Crawford who is my own lawyer to write you about this, and his letter is pinned right after Eliza's history. I may be could get a letter from one of the parsons only I don't know any of 'em and it don't seem as though any of the other members do.

Location and extent of country. I guess this is what you'd call mostly a form question that you have to ask small hunts located sort of next door to no place. In that Galloper Mag. I was telling you about it has hunts like Green Spring Valley, Myopia, Rose Tree, Orange County, and the like of that. Sounds like a seed catalogue. You wouldn't know where they were, but as you see from our letter paper we are right here in East Oil City. Then the extent of the country and the map. I don't know just how to handle this. I have pinned a map right after Judge Crawford's letter about our character, and I ran a red line in a circle about two hundred miles from East Oil City. Ed Beemis wanted me to take in the quarry up to Brillsburgh. Well I could of done it so far as Brillsburgh went, but as you can see I couldn't take in the same distance down south without running off the map and making the thing look bad. Of course Friend Maughn we don't want to have any less country than those Green Spring and those other fellows and if you think I should make it bigger I could take in the quarry and paste a piece of another map on the south and fix her all up.

Next is number of couples in kennels. Well since Joe Plimp's wife died he has lived alone out at the kennels.

Now about character of obstacles met with. I don't guess they're any worse than what other recognitioned hunts have. People don't pay up none too good. We have a locker room downstairs and things get kinda lively — you know — Saturday nights and the like of that, but nothing real bad. A lot of people's horses are always getting sore backs. I had to jolt over the country in a Ford two times last month hunting hounds that way all on account of my horse's back was so sore he wouldn't stand long enough to let me get on him. Leastways he made out it was sore, and the dogs don't do so good unless I'm right with them, and I liked to kill Tom McCarthy's kid on a pony by not seeing him all on account of half standing up in the car watching the dogs chasing somebody's cat. Of course there are a thousand of these sort of obstacles as you call them, but I don't suppose you want to hear them.

Now the next one — Disposition of land owners, is sure a stickler Mr. Maughn. We don't see what this has to do with fox dogs or hunting. I went over to the library and Eliza says the word disposition has a lot of meanings, and she says you probably want to know what becomes of the land owners when they kick in and the like of that. Well I don't know what to

say. I suppose just the same as any other place. I know that
when Phil Timmons came out hunting drunk and fell on the
State Road why everything was done bang up. That was
when we had that English huntsman I mentioned before, and
he was drunk too, and at the funeral he insisted on bringing
all the dogs and then he made them put Phil's whip and hat
in the coffin only they weren't Phil's but his brother's anyway, and that made a lot of row, and then he made them lead
Phil's horse with the funeral only he didn't own any. It was
rented and its knees were some bad from where it fell on the
State Road. Mr. Maughn there never was any Master of
Fox Dogs ever had a worse time with any huntsman than I
had with that Englishman. I sure got to tell you about it
some time. That history of Eliza's doesn't tell half of it because she don't know it.

The last one is, Name of huntsman. There is none now.
And about the nearest R.R. Station and places to wire and
mail and all the like of that, well that's another of those questions for those flower catalogue hunts. And how about this one
Elkridge — Why Mr. Maughn when I was up at Wyoming
there were more Elkridges than you can shake a stick at. Just
shoot me a wire, letter, package or anything else right here
to East Oil City. That's all you need.

I would like mighty well Friend Maughn to come on to
New York when the M.F.H.'s have their Annual Meeting
and dinner and the like of that. Please give me plenty notice.
I would sure like to meet the other M.F.H.'s from all over
and swap a few good stories. Talking about stories — now I
don't want to shove myself forward particilar as I will be a
new recognitioned member but I have some pretty good dia-
logue stuff what they always get me to do at dinners out here.

I thought I would tell you about it in case I could help you out. It's no good for mixed audiences. You know.

May be you could get me a room — something pretty good with a telephone and the like of that and here is another thing. I don't know my way about in New York so may be I had better bring my own stuff. You know. I could bring it in an extra suit case. Now there ain't a bit of use these days trying to entertain the whole world, so couldn't you just pick out a few M.F.H.'s you know. The president and some of our kind. I will have enough for that.

Would I need more than two pairs of white riding pants, say one pair for the day and the other pair for the dinners and those things? I guess that will be enough. Truth is we don't use 'em much out here. We don't ride in 'em but only for around the club Sundays and to have pictures took in and the like of that.

I don't think of much else I need to know right now. Let me know how you like Eliza's history. I'm kinda sorry about that English huntsman running off with Gus Emerley's wife. It don't just sound so good for a hunt club but I will explain all that when I see you. She wasn't so much anyway only that's just between us M.F.H's.

Here is something I came pretty near forgetting. When you write to me about coming down please be careful and send it to my office, 71 East Oil City Boulevard, and mark it Personal. Don't send it to the house. You know.

Just before I close and knowing you are always interested in hunting I'll tell you about a swell chase we had yesterday. We were running a gray fox when a jack jumped up and before we had run the jack more than a few hundred rods the dogs spied old Beemis's cat — sort of a tan colored cat —

well they ran her right into the old man's place and clean around his corn crib and gave her a good mauling all right, but didn't hurt her any — she just looked sort of wet and ruffed up you know. There was certainly lots doing, and an old bob-tailed hound we call "Casey" got away with a chicken. Beemis says two but I know better. I gave him half a buck. It was sure a lot of fun and a fine race. Well Friend Maughn I guess I had best close for now, so will say

Your truly,
OTTO.

P.S. Did I say somewhere in my letter that Mrs. Schmaltz would not be coming with me? Well she won't. You know.

I handed the papers back to Colonel Weatherford and he thrust them in his pocket. Later in the day as the Congressional was pulling out of Baltimore I said: "Colonel, if you could get hold of Eliza's history I would like to read about that English huntsman," but he made no reply.

CHAPTER IX.

The Rector of St. Timothy's

THE Rector of St. Timothy's, known throughout the parish as St. Timothy's in the Fields, had been awake since dawn. In truth he had seen each new day creep across Helmscote Heath towards the rectory for a full score of years, for it is a custom of old age to bear witness to the dawn.

On this particular Saturday morning he was loath to arise and face the day's events. On the other hand the thoughts and reflections which assailed him in bed seemed to make getting up the lesser evil. For the third time that morning he fumbled under his pillow for his watch, reached for his glasses, and consulted the time. There yet remained fifteen minutes before Mary Madden would come up with his hot water.

Fifty-two years ago he had received the living of St. Timothy's from the present Squire's father and moved into the rectory with his young wife, and Mary Madden had come to them as a maid of then eighteen years. During all these years Mary had brought up his hot water in the same tall pewter jug wrapped about with a piece of gray flannel. What continuity of service, he thought, and again his mind reverted to the unhappy recollections of the previous evening, and the equally trying drama to be enacted during the present day.

Tasker Oaks, the ever improvident village saddler, had died leaving a wife and three small children in perilous circumstances,— with no apparent means of support. The Rector had been to the "Hall" the evening before pleading with the Squire to permit the widow to occupy Willow Cottage rent-free for the balance of the year. Their talk had been extremely unpleasant for both of them. The Squire had been petulant and shown little sympathy or interest in the situation and had advanced his own increasing financial distress— tenants in arrears of rent, unemployment, mounting taxes, prohibitive costs of repairs, and the many demands of a newly acquired and fastidious wife. At eighty-one it is not easy to be combative and argumentative and the Rector came away with a feeling of having failed through his own impotency; yet he knew how much had been at stake for Nancy Oaks.

As he lay abed he concluded for the thousandth time that it was all due to the effects of the late War. To him his span of life divided itself into but two periods — the well-regulated, dependable, comprehensible years preceding the War — the years patterned by his ancestors, a time when one knew exactly what to expect from one's self, one's neighbors, and one's government — a pleasant era in which literature, art, music, sport and all social contacts changed and evolved with so slow a trend that one's susceptibilities were hardly aware of change. And then these post-War days — an uncongenial, incomprehensible period for old age to keep step with. An age in which he seemed to have little to offer which men and women wanted or appeared to need.

The Squire himself caused him untold concern. He had neglected the age-old precept that country should marry country, and as a result his lady had no insight into the problems of the estate. The "Hall" was but a place to visit periodically and to entertain in during the hunting season. Many of his parishioners lived in houses and cottages on the estate and the sympathy of the landlord for the needs and problems of the tenants was as necessary as the revolving of the seasons. Without this understanding help the ever-recurring misfortunes of life were often turned into tragedies.

Tasker Oaks was to be buried that morning, and in an effort to spare Nancy some expense the Rector had offered to drive her in his chaise to Abbots Appleby, nine miles away, where Tasker Oaks' kith and kind lay buried these three hundred years; Will Holcombe was to follow on with the coffin.

It was a long drive for his aged white horse and he knew well that before they would have cleared the village Nancy would ask him what the Squire had said, and he would have to tell her that she and the children would have to move, and there would be a long silence, and then she would ask what she and the bairns would do and where they would go, and he would have no answer for her and so would say that he would think it over. He would set himself to think it over but no thoughts would come to him, and to his humiliation and in spite of all his resolve, his old mind would get diverted by some inconsequential thing such as a bird flying overhead, yearling colts heckling each other in a pasture, or even a clump of brown winter weeds growing along the roadside,— and so he would finally say to Nancy that he would think things over for a few days and then come to see her.

To one in the late evening of life it is essential that civilization and its manifestations should not become too complex and incomprehensible, because one has not over-long in which to readjust one's views and faith; and yet this matter of

Nancy Oaks was perplexing in the extreme. He could not reconcile his mind to a civilization which could neglect so splendid an institution as Nancy and her children, for to him she typified the very best of rural England.

He heard Mary Madden coming upstairs with the hot water and wondered whether it was only the reflection of his own thoughts which made her steps sound slow and dull that morning. He heard her enter the bathroom, pull back the curtains, do the same in his dressing room, and start the fire; then come to his door, rap and say, "It's a quarter past eight, Sir, and a pleasant day, only a mite overcast."

As he started to shave he noticed that the new Hunt fixture card had been propped up against the mirror, held in place by a diminutive bronze figure of the great sire, *Stockwell*, which had served this purpose for half a century. This kindly little act of arranging the fixture cards, which Mary persisted in, always amused and pleased him. It was an effort on Mary's part to suggest that he had not actually given up hunting, but, rather, was not going out that season.

From habit he invariably consulted the card each morning to see where hounds were meeting, and to call to mind the scene as it would be enacted, and would ever and anon say to himself in good part, "Well if I *were* hunting I could not go out today. There is too much to be done." On mornings when the weather precluded any possibility of hounds going out, Mary would say at breakfast, "There will be no hunting today, Sir," just as though he might have planned to hunt, and he would say, "No, Mary, no hunting today. Perhaps it will be better by the next hunting day."

Five years ago on his seventy-sixth birthday he had formally abandoned the sport. That day had marked his sixty-fifth year in the field, for he had had his first day to hounds on his eleventh birthday. How well he remembered that first day. His grandfather had been Master of Hounds and had given him a new shilling for jumping his pony over a goodly brook. Then his memory reverted to the day five years ago, his last day to hounds, and how people of all degrees had expressed regret that he was giving up the sport, and young and old had said kindly things of good cheer to him. Before starting downstairs he glanced at the card and saw that the fixture for the day was Thornhill Upper Bridge at 11 a.m.

After attending to his mail and one or two matters pertaining to the morrow's service he called for Nancy Oaks and together they started their sombre drive to Abbotts Appleby. Their conversation had been much as he had feared it would be, and he had been of little present help. He had known Nancy since she was a wee tot playing up and down the village street, and her burdens and perplexities weighed heavily upon him.

After passing through Wedmere Cross they mounted the long hill which leads over the Peak of Medford. On the summit the Rector rested his white cob and waited for Will Holcombe's slower horse to come up with them.

Looking to the west he could follow the valley of the river Tro until it narrowed into a gorge five miles away and disappeared to the north around Holderness Head. "Thornhill Upper Bridge at 11 a.m.," flashed through his mind. If Tim Templer had found in West End Spinny, hounds might now be running some place in the valley between Holderness Head and Medford Bottom. He stood up in the chaise and peered long and intently. He was a tall, slightly stooped, frail man with white hair, and there was a shade of longing in his fine face.

As he stood thus scanning the valley, the pale, wintry sun disentangled itself from masses of gray clouds and filled the valley with light, and there, some two miles up the vale, was the glint of scarlet and presently he distinguished hounds racing on towards him. He started the cob on its tortuous course down the hill, and as the banks were high no further view was had of hounds, but as the chaise approached Medford Bottom, which is a mile wide at that point, he heard hounds on the right and coming towards them. He focused his eyes on the long straight road in front of him for the fox was bound to cross somewhere in the bottom.

Of a sudden he was startled by the horn of a great motor bus, hastily pulled to the side of the road and the bus sped past, leaving the air rancid with fumes. He again fixed his eyes on the road and saw a small red object slip from the hedge row into the road and run in the air-fouled wake of the fast disappearing bus. Smart — very smart — mused the Rector. That will worry them.

He brought the cob to a standstill to wait for the field to cross the road and gallop on wishing to spare Nancy any contact with the Hunt, but as he waited he watched the fox. On and on it ran. Never, thought the Rector, will hounds unsnarl that line and, in such mild manner as is permissible to a rector of advanced age, he asked for divine condemnation upon cement roads, internal combustion engines, all standard and other brands of petrol, and in particular the fumes left by each — then he saw the fox turn left-handed and disappear through a break in the hedge.

The Rector heard hounds carry the line with fine cry to the edge of the road — then there was silence. First one hound and then another entered the road, and threw their

The Rector views the fox.

heads right and left, but without a whimper. Some of the more impetuous hounds given to wider casts, carried their search across the road. He knew that Tim Templer would let them try it alone before he helped them, and so hounds sought for the thin thread of scent growing ever thinner with each passing moment.

The humble funeral cortège was concealed from the field by a growth of alder bushes. The Rector of St. Timothy's was too heavy of heart at that moment to feel in tune with the hunt. What sympathy he felt was all for the hounds. They were baffled as he was baffled through the innovations of the times. He rebelled at the thought of exposing Nancy in her grief to the countryside at play, but twice Nancy had asked him in her gentle, faltering voice if they might not be late. He knew that Tim Templer would make every conceivable cast before he would abandon the fox, and so he finally decided to drive on and be through with it.

He put the gray cob in action, beckoned Will Holcombe to follow on, and so came into view of the field. They were standing a hundred yards or more from the road watching Tim cast his hounds. A hundred scarlet coats and shimmering silk hats. As the chaise came into view Tim stopped his horse and ceased talking to his hounds. The Squire said to him, "Tim, I have no doubt the Rector knows what became of that fox, but who would dare ask him now?" But Tim was not listening to the M.F.H. The narrow, lively slits in his weather-beaten face that served him as eyes were staring at the chaise. The gray cob was creeping his deliberate way across the long straight cement road while Will Holcombe's aged sorrel mare followed with her doleful burden.

Attracted by his huntsman's gazing, the Squire looked over

at the Rector and saw that his round black hat was being held far aloft. The Squire removed his velvet cap and stood thus until the Rector might again replace his hat. On and on the chaise proceeded until it was far beyond the field and still the black hat remained aloft. The members of the hunt went back to their chattering, but Tim Templer's narrow eyes were twinkling and the Master continued to hold his cap in his hand. He too was staring. Then of a sudden Tim heard him say, "I have it. By God, what a prince the old man is!" The chaise at last reached a place where a break or gap appeared in the hedge at the left of the road, and they saw the round black hat tilt far out to the left, and then return to its owner's head. Master and huntsman smiled at each other, and Tim called his hounds to him.

When the chaise disappeared from view an impatient huntsman took his hounds at a gallop to a break in the hedge, and as the Rector turned a bend in the road he heard hounds open and knew they were flying on; in spite of himself a gentle smile broke over his deep-lined face.

It was dusk when Tim Templer and his two whippers-in passed through the village to the kennels. The Rector was returning from dropping a letter in the post. At sight of him Tim stopped his horse and removing his cap, said, "Please, Sir, if you're to be at home and could find it convenient, Sir, I would like to speak with you a piece as soon as I see to the hounds."

Within the hour the huntsman was in the rectory library and telling of the greatest run in the history of the hunt, and how the fox had run eight and twenty miles, and how the Squire had said on the way home that there was little to choose in distance between their run and the great Waterloo

Run of the Pychley in '62 when they found in Waterloo Gorse and had to stop hounds after three hours and forty-five minutes close to Blaiston, except that he and the Squire had killed their fox. In his enthusiasm Tim unfolded the course hounds ran and opened a great panorama of country which his listener followed mile upon mile.

Of a sudden Tim stopped, "Excuse me, Sir. I didn't come to tell you all this. I clean forgot myself. I came for something else."

"Timothy Templer, never interrupt a story like that. Particularly that kind of a story. Where did you kill?"

"On the edge of a bit of gorse just afore the river turns to slip away into Fernsworth Fenns. We were well into Mr. Stackpole's country. The furthest from home ever I've been on a horse. There was only the Squire and that American gentleman, Mr. Weatherford, what has the Grange at Dunmorrow, with me when we killed and we waited there a spell and the gentlemen kept coming up for as long as ever we waited for they were strung back all the ways to the ford at Weston, and never a second horse to be found when they were needed. If there was a half-bred horse within five miles of the kill I never saw him.

"What I came to say, Sir, was as how the gentlemen were uncommonly generous with me on account of how it was such a grand run and gave me most six pounds, and, Sir, I was thinking some of poor Tasker and his widow and them children. He was never much of a one to save a shilling was Tasker, but we was friends a goodish long time. He did the fixing of the tack up at the kennels. I was thinking as how I'd like to give you three pounds if you could find a way to get it to Nancy, for she would never take it from me, Sir, and

Slem Whimple and the Connors boy who are whipping to me this season say as how they would like to add ten shillings apiece, so that's four pounds, and here it is, Sir, if you'd be pleased to take it, and I must be getting along. *Old Crusader* that I rode today wouldn't as much as take a sniff at his oats and I'll be having a look at him. I don't know as how you'd like to have me mention it, Sir. Maybe you wouldn't, but you were a powerful help to me today, Sir. The smell of that motor bus and the way the wind was blowing on the cement road made it pretty hard for the hounds. Good night, Sir, and thank you."

The morning of the Third Sunday in Lent commenced as all Sunday mornings had commenced in the rectory of St. Timothy's in the Fields time out of mind, except that the Rector himself was not quite in the "pink." The long cold drive of the day before had been somewhat of a strain on him and he felt stiff and draggy as he walked across the lawn to the church. Then he forgot the memorandum of announcements he was to make and had to retrace his steps. When he reached the vestry room the choir was assembled and ready to commence the processional and he could hear the organ playing the last bars of Bach's Chorale, *What Tongue Can Tell Thy Greatness, Lord.*

The verger helped him on with his cassock and surplice as he had done for so many years, and he heard the organ commence the grand old marching hymn, *Ride on, Ride on to Victory.* The verger in his black robe stepped forward and opened the heavy oak door leading to the church and the Morning Service of St. Timothy's in the Fields had commenced.

How well he knew the sight that would meet his eyes. A

scant half of the pews would be occupied and these princi-
pally by old people from up and down the village street with
here and there an elderly spinster from the country houses.

He followed the words of the hymn and did not look up
until he had reached his place in the choir stalls, and then let
his eye wander off over his congregation. To his amazement
there was not an empty pew and scarce an unoccupied seat.

A great alarm spread over him. He had been conscious
lately of many evidences of a fast failing memory. Could he
by any chance have miscalculated the period since Ash Wednesday? Could this be Easter Sunday? Within his remembrance the church had never been so filled except at Easter.
It was with infinite relief that he finally fixed it in his mind
that it was but the Third Sunday in Lent.

By the time he had finished reading the First Lesson appointed for that Sunday he had regained his composure, but
to his further amazement he kept discovering one foxhunting person after another in the congregation. For the first
time in many months the Squire and his lady were in the family pew. By the conclusion of the service he had discovered
practically all of the first-flight, hard-riding members of the
Hunt.

When the choir again reached the vestry room and were
singing the last verse of the Recessional the verger closed the
batten door, which caused the singing to sound as though it
came from afar off and the Morning Service was over. The
verger handed him the green cloth bag containing the offering and he took his perplexed way home, but even as he did
so he could not free his mind from the thought that the day
must have been set apart in people's minds as a memorial the
very nature of which had slipped his memory and that surely

there was something he should have made reference to in the service.

Upon reaching his study he proceeded to arrange the contents of the green bag upon his desk preparatory to counting it. In the bag he discovered a large envelope addressed to him in handwriting which he recognized as that of Mr. Merrill Meredith, a substantial land-owner, a keen sportsman and an old friend. He opened the envelope which he found to contain a letter from Meredith and another from the Squire.

The Meredith letter ran:

A group of your old friends dining together at John Weatherford's last evening following the longest and most spectacular run of this or any other season for our hounds talked long and affectionately of you, and wishing to give more tangible proof of their regard subscribed the sum of sixty-five pounds to a fund to be used as you may think best in the relief of any case or cases of distress in our village. My check for this amount is enclosed.

With expressions of warm personal regard, I remain,

Very sincerely yours,

Merrill Meredith.

The Squire wrote:

My dear Dominie:

I tender my apologies and regrets for the affair of Friday evening. Please accept them. How many times I wonder have you forgiven and overlooked since I was a wee shaver. I know I am a continual disappointment to you. Please say to Nancy Oaks that she may occupy the cottage rent free for as long

as you feel she should have it. If anything untowards happens to her or the children and I not be available I have instructed Smithers to honor any demands you may make on
him for this purpose.

Please don't take it amiss but you were magnificent, really
magnificent, yesterday on the Medford road.

The Rector had long since finished his dinner yet sat
quietly alone in his armchair at the head of the table and
peace and contentment were in his face. When Mary entered
he asked her to hand him a cigar. "There it is in your very
hand, Sir, and you aturning it around and around." "Oh
yes, so it is Mary. I was thinking of something else. And
Mary, would you send the cook's little boy over to Nancy
Oaks to say I would like to see her here just before the Ves-
per Service, and Mary please bring me a scrap of paper. My
memory is not very good — any little piece — an old envelope will do."

When on Monday morning the verger was tidying up and
putting the books away in the chancel he picked up an envelope addressed to the rector from Hemple & Mellick, Coal,
Wood, Feed and Building Supplies, and was about to dispose
of it when he saw a note on the back.

"I want them to sing *Faith, Perfect Faith* at this evening's
service."

CHAPTER X.

A Night at the Old Bergen County Race Track

I HAD arranged to meet Colonel Weatherford at his club at four o'clock, motor to the country with him and hunt in the morning. Upon reaching the club I found a note advising me that the Colonel would be detained but telling me to take his car and that he would be up on the seven o'clock train. I was to give his man, Albert, whom I would find in the car, a message about having the Colonel met at the train, and regarding the horse he wished to hunt in the morning. I located the car and started for the country.

I had bought an afternoon paper which I read while we were motoring through Central Park. The sporting page contained one of those disagreeable accounts from the race track telling of a sponge having been found in a horse's nostril. This incident reminded me of something about which I rather wanted to learn. Albert was sitting in the back of the car with me, the front seat having been given over to a steamer trunk, so I said, "Albert, an old friend of Colonel Weatherford whom I met the other day asked me if I had ever heard about a little run-in which the Colonel had years ago with some bookmakers over at the old Bergen County track in New Jersey. What was the story." "Well, Sir," said Albert, "it's not a thing I like to talk about because it puts me in a very bad light, Sir, but it was so long ago I guess it doesn't matter now." Albert then told me the story.

A few years after I took service with Colonel Weatherford he became interested in flat racing. At the time you speak about, Sir, he had four horses in training over at the old Bergen County track in New Jersey. There were some very rough characters around that track in those days, and the gambling was pretty heavy.

One of the Colonel's horses was a brown colt he had imported from France called *Le Grand Chên* by the English horse, *White Oak*. You know how the Colonel is, Sir, about certain of his horses and hunting dogs. Every once in a while he takes a very particular liking to some animal and when he does he puts great store by him. Well *Le Grand Chên* was one of them and you couldn't blame the Colonel for feeling the way he did about that colt. Of course, Sir, I'm not a horse-man, but it didn't take a horseman to admire that horse. He was a big seal brown three-year-old with white on three of his legs, a white star on his forehead, and the largest finest eye I ever saw on any horse. When you opened his box he would turn his head, look you square in the eye like some people do, then walk up and visit and stand looking at you as long as ever you stayed with him. The boys who took care of the colt were very sweet on him because he seemed to be always trying to do just what you wanted him to do.

There was one big important stake to be run for at that meeting called the North Jersey Stakes and the Colonel was a deal set on winning it with this colt. He had come down from Massachusetts and was staying a fortnight at the old Holland House in New York, and had brought me down with him. He thought a powerful lot of that hotel and even now says there was never a hotel like it.

Well, it came along to a Friday morning. The stake was to be run the next day. The Colonel had spent Thursday at the track and said to me when he came home that the colt was tight, should win in a canter, and that a pot of money had been wagered on him to win. The Colonel was in fine spirits about his chances. I had never seen him so enthusiastic about anything as he was about that colt that evening.

About eight o'clock Friday morning he sent for me. I bought a morning paper for him, went to his room, found what he wanted for breakfast, ordered it, and was laying out his clothes when he said, "Albert, what is that on the floor over by the door." I went over to the door, picked up a soiled mussy looking envelope, looked at it, saw the Colonel's name scrawled across it in lead pencil and handed it to him. I returned to the bureau and was starting to pull out a drawer when I heard the Colonel jump out of bed. As he did so he said, "I'm in a hurry. Telephone about breakfast," and went in the bathroom where I heard a big commotion going on. All the spigots in the place must have been turned on at once. He was out in jig time and into his clothes. He paid little attention to his breakfast and as soon as he had finished he gathered up his hat, gloves and stick, said he was going to the track, and started out of the door. Then he turned and told me to stay in the hotel and be where the telephone operator could reach me. I was a good deal troubled, Sir, for the Colonel had acted quite upset. While he was dressing he had walked over to the window and stood looking out over Fifth Avenue with his hands behind his back, and kept tapping the floor with his foot. They weren't just taps, Sir, for his foot came down hard and deliberate like. I put things to rights and went downstairs.

As I was passing the head porter's desk he called me over, took me into his back office, shut the door and said, "Albert, what's gone wrong with your Governor's horse? I have a bet on him and all the boys in the house are on him. Come on now — be a good fellow — what's up?" I told him I hadn't heard a thing except that the Colonel was very sweet on the colt and had told me only the night before that he expected to win with him. Then it was my turn so I said, "Jim, now you come across." He sort of fiddled about and then said, "Well, Albert, all I know is that a pretty smart guy who doesn't often get burned went out of his way to send word to me at six o'clock this morning to lay off or if it was too late then to hedge and take care of myself."

I stayed in the hotel all day but nothing happened. Then at four o'clock a call came, a voice I didn't recognize said I was to come to the track right away, meet the Colonel at his stable and get supper on the way.

Our four horses were in a small, detached stable at the end of a long line of boxes. When I arrived I found the Colonel entirely alone and sitting on a bale of hay which he had placed in front of the box where *Le Grand Chên* always stood. There was no one else in or around the stable. He asked me if I had had supper. I told him I had. Then he said, "Albert I want you to sit here and watch these four stalls and stay here until either Pat Dwyer or I come to relieve you. You are not to permit any one to enter any part of the stable nor even approach the stall doors. I have telephoned Dwyer to catch the first train from Boston and he will be here in the morning. (Pat Dwyer was the Colonel's head groom then as he is now.) I will rely on you not to fall asleep nor to leave the place for an instant. I have discharged every one connected with the stable." He started to move away but came back and, handing me a pistol, said, "Should you be molested this may be serviceable in summoning assistance. Do not use it for any other purpose if you can avoid it, and Albert I don't think I would turn my back to that swamp. Good night."

As I said our stable was off by itself. In the rear a dreary looking field strewn with rocks and bushes stretched away to the west. To the north and about three hundred feet away lay a patch of woods with a lane running through it leading to some shanties where they said a good deal of gambling and other things went on. In front of the stable the ground sloped down to a swamp with cat-tails and alder bushes growing in it. The nearest other stable was three or four hundred feet to the south. It was close to dusk when the Colonel left me, for it was the Fall Meeting and the days were short. I made myself as comfortable as might be on the bale of hay and sat there watching it grow dark. Pretty soon lanterns began to show at the different stables and I could hear box stalls and tack room doors being closed and saw the lights moving up and down the long rows of stables. Before long the lanterns became fewer and fewer as the boys went away to their suppers and for the night. It became very quiet. After about an hour I saw a lantern coming down the long line of boxes. It stopped at the stable next to ours and I knew from the sounds that followed that some of the swipes had started a crap game in the tack room. I was glad of it for the place didn't seem so lonesome. They played a long time. Once I heard a horse coughing and one of the boys took the lantern and went into the horse's box. The game ended about midnight. The boys came out, closed the tack room door and the lantern slowly disappeared. I sat a few minutes staring into the dark, then walked to the end of our stable and looked over towards the track and the rest of the stabling. Everything was dark except for one light away off, maybe half a mile away and as I watched even it disappeared. I climbed back on the bale of hay and sat there. Once I heard a horse in a distant stable kicking the side of his box and it sounded sort of good to me. I kept wishing our horses would move about or do something. I took the pistol out of my pocket and turned it over in my hand the way you do.

Of a sudden I heard something moving in the swamp. The sound was so faint I could hardly hear it and couldn't have told any one what kind of a sound it was yet I knew something was moving. I slipped off the bale and tip-toed slowly towards the edge of the swamp. Sometimes I couldn't hear anything, then there would be the sound of feet moving in the soft ground. Once or twice I heard the dry stems of the cat-tails clicking against each other. I started to take a step backward when a clump of cat-tails rustled so close to me that I instinctively raised the pistol. Something was coming straight towards me. I didn't know whether to stand steady or move back towards the stable when a goat walked out of the swamp and went off towards one of the stables.

I returned to the stable and was laying the pistol down when I saw something white on the hay. Putting my hand on it I found it to be a piece of paper. I had had no paper in my pocket and I knew there had been nothing on the hay when I walked over to the edge of the swamp.

I don't know how it was, Sir, but that piece of paper gave me sort of a turn. I didn't like to strike a match, but it seemed like I just had to find out what the paper was so I crept up to the far end of the stable, went maybe ten feet around the corner, turned my back on the swamp, unbuttoned my coat, ducked my head down like you see people trying to light a match in a wind, struck a match right close to me, looked at the paper and read, "Get out of here while you can." I blew out the match, listened a minute, then went back to the hay. A clock away off somewhere struck two o'clock. I heard the brown colt get up on his feet and walk around his box. The handle of the water pail rattled so I knew he was taking a drink.

It's odd, Sir, isn't it, the sort of things that come into your head at times like those. I got to thinking of the games of cribbage I used to play every night at the Holland House with Jim the porter in his snug little office. I hadn't rightly thought much of that office before, but sitting out there in the dark it seemed a cozy, safe kind of place. Then I got to thinking of the Colonel's fine home away up in Massachusetts where he lived.

Of a sudden I felt a cold damp blast of air on my face. A fresh east wind had blown up and was driving big clouds of fog in from the sea. In less than a minute it turned dreadful cold. Mr. Pendleton, Sir, I've been cold lots of times but never anything like I was then. I didn't have any overcoat and only a light suit. I began to shake and my teeth to chatter. It didn't seem like I could stand it. I wanted to go in with one of the horses but the Colonel had said he didn't want any of the boxes opened or the horses disturbed. I tried our tack room thinking may be to find a blanket but the door was locked. All of a sudden I remembered that before it had grown dark I had seen some blankets or coolers hanging on a line back of the stable next to ours, and hoped that maybe they had been left out all night. It was pitch dark but I thought I could walk right to 'em even in the fog so started. I walked with my hands out in front of me and had good luck for pretty soon I touched a corner of the stable and knew that the line was about thirty feet to the rear of the building. It took a good deal of groping about to find the line but I finally brushed up against the blankets, took two of them and started back. Mr. Pendleton, Sir, I don't know what ever I did to get twisted about after that. I thought I was headed straight for our stable but after walking a short way the ground started to slope down very steep like. I stopped a second then took a couple of more steps, but the footing felt soft and slippery. I had gotten twisted around and had walked straight for the swamp. I stood and listened a spell but there was no sound from our stable. Then I figured out that if I walked along the edge of the swamp about three hundred feet, then turned sharp to the left, and could walk a straight line I would hit some part of the stable. I have never seen anything like the dark of that night. It seemed as though you had to shove the fog away before you could move. I started walking, feeling my way every step and trying to keep on the edge of the swamp.

It's an odd thing, Sir, how for no reason that you know about you can tell when things aren't right. I had been pretty good up to then but all of a sudden I began to feel jumpy. I had walked maybe half the distance along the swamp and had stopped to calculate about where I should be when of a sudden I heard a footstep and some one crossed right in front of me. I froze where I stood and reached for the pistol. It was on the bale of hay. Who ever had been moving had stopped. A horse over at our stable struck the side of his box the way they do sometimes when getting to their feet in a hurry. It didn't seem like I could walk straight ahead knowing that someone was standing there waiting so I made a quarter turn to the left and trusted to luck to hit the stable. I raised my foot, took a step and was just raising the other foot when I heard a pistol being cocked. I stopped short. The ground was sticky and pretty soon I heard some one shifting his weight from one foot to another. Then I heard a low whistle from some where out in the swamp. That settled it. I knew then that I had to get to our stable no matter what happened. I gulped and started. I walked maybe ten paces right smart then stopped short to listen. Some one was following close behind me. I dropped the blankets and stepped quickly to one side. Some one tripped over the blankets but went on. I couldn't stand the thing any longer. I knew where the stable ought to be so I clenched my fists and ran for it as fast as ever I could run. I had gone maybe a hundred feet when something struck me a blow on the head that knocked me to the ground. I tried to get to my feet but was sick and dizzy like. I knew I would be hit again and should get up but couldn't. Then I heard a noise near me and listened. It was a horse getting upon his feet. I had hit my head on one of the posts of our stable. I reached out my hand, took hold of the post, got to my feet and listened. There was not a sound to be heard. I walked over to the bale of hay, found it against the colt's box, and the pistol where I had left it. Everything seemed all right. I picked up the pistol, cocked it and sat bolt upright listening and staring into the fog.

The half hours and hours tolled off but I never heard another sound from the swamp or any place else. Finally it commenced to grow light and I could see people moving about at the different stables and saw a colt being led over to the track for an early trial. I was mighty glad, Sir, to see the end of that night.

At a quarter to eight the Colonel and Pat Dwyer drove up in a cab. Pat whipped off his coat and started feeding and watering, while the Colonel inspected the horses. I was lending Pat a hand when of a sudden I heard the Colonel call me. He was standing at *Le Grand Chên's* box. He closed the box and walked over to meet me. Never before nor since, Sir, have I seen him look as he did that moment. He started to speak to me but instead called to Dwyer and pointed to the colt's box, then turned his back on me and walked off a few paces. Finally he turned, came back and faced me. It's wonderful, Sir, how he can hide what he is feeling and thinking. His face had entirely changed from what it was when he stood at the colt's box. Then I heard Pat Dwyer come out of the colt's box and say, "Good God a'mighty, Mr. John."

The Colonel looked at me for what seemed an age, then said in a quiet voice, "Albert, did you leave the stable last night?" "Yes, Sir," I said, "I walked over to that clothes line over there back of that stable. It was very cold, Sir, and I wanted a blanket. It was about three o'clock." He turned and studied the clothes line. "How long did it take you?" "Well, Sir," I said, "I didn't think it would take more than three or four minutes but it was very dark and I couldn't find the blankets right away, then when I did find them I got some mixed up and twisted around in trying to get back. It might have taken me ten minutes or may be fifteen."

He didn't say anything for perhaps half a minute, then

continued more to himself than to me, "Three or four minutes to get a horse blanket if you were cold. Who the devil wouldn't. They thought he had left for good. If he had come back sooner they would have got him. If he hadn't gone they might have got him. I had no right to leave him here alone." He walked over to the edge of the swamp and stood a long time examining the ground, then he deliberately stepped into the soft clay at the fringe of the swamp with one foot, held his foot there a while, came back to the stable, sat down on the bale, and went to studying the muddy shoe. He called Dwyer to him and they had a serious talk about the colt. It struck me as wonderful the way the Colonel took the whole thing. Dwyer asked him for a piece of paper and wrote out a prescription. Then the Colonel again sat looking at the mud on his shoe as though he had nothing else in the world to think about. He handed me the prescription and told me to get it filled. I asked him if I might look at the colt, but he said he did not want him disturbed.

When I got back to the stable with the medicine Pat Dwyer was doing up the horses while the Colonel sat on the bale reading the morning paper.

About half-past eleven I heard some one come up and speak to the Colonel. I turned around and saw it to be a man by the name of Jake Katz. This Katz was one of the best known gamblers around the track in those days but nobody half way respectable would be seen speaking to him. I don't guess there are any of his kind around these days. He was the leader of a group of bookmakers who had made a pile of money through being mixed up with a chain of pool rooms and in other ways. This Katz was the brains of the outfit. I was surprised to see him down at our stable talking to the

Colonel. They were standing outside of the tack room where I was cleaning a bridle for Pat and I heard Katz say, "Well, Colonel, and how is that grand colt of yours. I declare he is the best looking three-year-old I've seen out in ten years and he moves just as sweet as he looks. He is the kind of a horse I like to have a look at once in awhile just to keep my eye in. Could I have a peek at him?"

The Colonel smiled at him as though he was his very best friend and said, "I'd be delighted to have you look at him Mr. Katz. I appreciate the complimentary things you have said about the colt. We are a bit short handed today but, of course we will show him to you. Albert slip the blanket off the brown colt." I went to the colt's box, opened the door and removed his blanket. Mr. Pendleton, Sir, I couldn't understand how the Colonel could ever do such a thing. That was the first time I had seen the colt that morning and there he was standing in one corner with his head down pretty near to his knees, his eyes glassy, and when I took the blanket off I could see that he was having a hard time to breathe. I wished I had never seen him.

The Colonel and Katz stood at the door looking into the box. Neither of them spoke. Then I suppose Katz felt that he ought to say something as long as he had asked to see the colt so he said, "That's one of the best balanced colts that ever looked through a bridle," and continued to look at him. Then I saw the Colonel do a very queer thing, Sir. On the excuse of lighting his pipe he stepped back of Katz, struck a match, but did not use it, then rejoined Katz. You see, Sir, I was looking at the Colonel because I was hoping he would signal me to put the blanket back for never in my life had I seen such a sick animal. As soon as he had rejoined Katz he said,

"Mr. Katz, I suppose I should have some sort of a wager on my horse for this afternoon's race. I understand the talent doesn't think as much of him as they did. They don't approve of my discharging my trainer just before an important race. I am told that the odds have lengthened very much on the colt this morning. I admit the horse does not look as fit as I would wish him but still I am sentimental about him. What are you quoting on him or rather what will you quote me on him?" Katz cleared his throat. This was not what he had expected. "Well, Mr. Weatherford," he said, "I don't know. They say the colt has a turn of speed and can go the route. On the other hand it looks like there would be a big field. I could make it 6 to 1." "No," said the Colonel. "That would not interest me." Katz turned and looked at the colt again and stood looking at him, then said, "Mr. Weatherford, I have never had the pleasure of doing any business with you. I would like to make a start. I will make it 10 to 1." Without a second's hesitation the Colonel took out his wallet and handed Katz four five-hundred-dollar bills. There was no mistake about Katz being taken back by the size of the wager. He held the bills in his hand, turned around, looked closely at the colt, folded the bills, put them in his pocket, said, "All right, Mr. Weatherford, much obliged," and went off. I had been putting the blanket back on the colt while they were talking and came out of the box just as Katz started away. The Colonel was standing with his feet apart, swinging his walking stick behind his back, and following Katz with his eye. I also looked and there on the back of each of Katz's heels was a dab of light yellow clay. When Katz was out of sight the Colonel put his stick in a corner of the stable, sat down on the bale of hay, asked me if I would get something which would take the clay off his heels, took a magazine out of his pocket, and started to read.

Mr. Pendleton, Sir, it seemed like I had enough to worry about and feel bad about that morning without the Colonel making that $2000 bet. To be game was all right but I couldn't see the use of fighting after you were licked. Next to being sore at myself I was most sore at Pat Dwyer. I knew he must have told the Colonel that he could fix the colt up in an hour or two so he could run. It seemed to me just like one of those Irish superstitions. You know, Sir, one of those quack remedies he most likely got from a witch and all that. He was in the colt's box fussing with him every ten minutes. Why I had brought enough stuff and paraphernalia from the drug store to start a horse hospital with. I couldn't see how a man like the Colonel could be fooled by such rubbish because even if the colt did get all right before the race he was bound to be right weak.

At noon time the Colonel told me I would not be needed until just before our race so to go to lunch and gave me some telegrams to send for him. As I was about to start he called me and handed me a hundred dollar bill saying, "Albert, put this on our colt for Pat and yourself, but mind you lay it only with one of these four bookmakers." He handed me a corner torn from the morning newspaper with four names written on it. One of them was Katz.

I never spent three such bad hours in my life. The only thing I could think of was that fine colt over at our stable. How sick he looked, how bad he must feel. Then of the Colonel and Dwyer trying to cure him in time to race, of how much the Colonel thought of the colt, how his heart had been sure set on winning this big stake, but worst of all I was thinking of my going off in the fog to get those blankets. I didn't feel good when I was at the stable but it seemed like I felt worse when I was away from it.

I went back to the stable just before it was time for the horses entered in the stake to start for the saddling paddock. As I approached the stable I saw Dwyer leading *Le Grand Chên* up and down all covered up with a cooler. Certainly Dwyer seemed to have done him some good for he looked brighter in the eye and walked free but even so I couldn't understand why the Colonel, who didn't need the money, would ever ask a horse he was fond of to run in that condition. He wasn't my horse but it didn't seem like I could watch him strain and struggle the way they have to. I heard the Colonel tell Dwyer they would wait until the last minute because he didn't want the colt standing in the paddock any longer than he could help. When time was up we started, Dwyer leading the colt, the Colonel and I following. As we approached the paddock the Colonel called me over close to him and said, "Albert this horse may look a little better to some people when we take his cooler off than they are expecting. I am going to hold him and Dwyer saddle him. The instant the cooler comes off you look sharp. Stand back of me and keep your eyes open. I don't want any one coming within arms length of this colt. Don't worry about insulting any one or getting arrested. I will take care of you."

Dwyer found a corner in the paddock where we could be off by ourselves, slipped the cooler off and started to saddle. It wasn't half a minute before I saw a small group of people huddled together and looking our way. Four or five hard-looking customers were even pointing at the colt. Then one of them slipped under the rail and went up to two men who

[169]

were saddling a horse and pretty soon they all began to edge up towards us. The Colonel had seen the whole thing and immediately led *Le Grand Chên* away. Then the bugle blew. On the way to the track the Colonel took one side of the colt's bridle and Dwyer the other. As soon as the colt was safe on the track I hurried off to get a seat.

I couldn't rightly make up my mind whether I wanted to watch the race or not but anyway I went on with the crowd. There were twelve starters and the distance was a mile and a quarter. The field got off to a prompt start but for the first quarter I couldn't find our colt, then the field commenced to string out and I found him. There were three horses out front, then came a horse called *St. Anthony*, a good horse that won a lot of races after that. He was running alone right back of the leaders. A couple of lengths back of *St. Anthony* were four horses bunched together. Then *Le Grand Chên* running by himself and three horses trailing him. I didn't know a lot about horses in those days, but it seemed to me we must have had the gamest colt in the world for even in the condition he was in he was out-running three horses. At the end of the next quarter one of the leading horses had dropped back. *St. Anthony* had moved up and there were now four horses back of our brown colt. They ran this way until the three-quarter pole, then our horse moved up a little closer to the horses right in front of him and they started around the turn. There was a man standing next to me with a pair of field glasses. He must have seen that I was mighty interested in that race for he said, "Have a look," so I took the glasses. As I was saying, Sir, they were rounding the turn. The horses in front of our colt ran wide. Then I could hardly believe what I saw through the glasses. Of a sudden the boy on *Le Grand Chên* took him close to the rail and shot him through. It was wonderful, Sir. I was returning the glasses to the man when I heard some one back of me say, "What the h—— is that brown colt doing?" and some one whispered "Shut up, it's all right, I tell you." I couldn't help turning around. The first speaker was the man I had seen slip under the paddock fence when we were saddling. The horses had passed the mile and were well started on the last quarter. *St. Anthony* in front by three lengths, then a chestnut colt and *Le Grand Chên* at the chestnut's quarters. Then something happened that made me so mad, Sir, that I could hardly look at the race for the boy on our colt drew his whip and went to it and he did go to it. It was terrible for I was just thinking how fine and game the colt had been and to see any one hit him seemed more than I could stand. The boy hadn't more than touched the colt when he shot past the chestnut horse as though he had been tied. Why Mr. Pendleton he overhauled *St. Anthony* like he was standing still. But *St. Anthony* had a lot in reserve. You see his jockey had been caught napping. Our colt caught him in a couple of strides but then the race started. Both boys were at their bats. They fought it out inch by inch. The crowd was roaring and everywhere around me I kept hearing, "Come on you *Anthony*, come on you *Anthony*." Neither colt would give up. They were a couple of lions to take punishment and the boys knew it and kept sailing into them. When they were three strides from the finish you couldn't tell which was in front. Neither colt could gain, and they finished just that way. No one in the stand knew who had won. There were about 15,000 people at the race and they all stood up watching the board, then I saw our colt's number put up. Think of it, Sir.

I hurried as fast as ever I could to get to the Colonel and the colt and Pat Dwyer. I've heard, Sir, about people throwing their arms around horses' necks and all that. Well I don't know but what if there had been nobody around maybe I would have done the same. I wanted to go back to our stable with them all, but the Colonel handed me a note he had written to one of the stewards and told me to find him and give it to him. I knew the gentleman well by sight but it took me half an hour to find him, then I went to the stable. I didn't walk, Sir, I ran. When I got there the colt's box was open, the Colonel was standing at the door looking in and Pat Dwyer was in the box and down on his knees doing something to the colt's legs. Mr. Pendleton, after seeing the way that horse ran it was pitiful to see what the race had taken out of him. He was standing there absolutely exhausted, with his head way down, and you could see the blanket going up and down as he tried to breathe. It struck me that human beings didn't have any right to do such things with animals. As I said Dwyer was working on the horse's legs. He had a can of something and a roll of cotton. He would wet the cotton and rub it up and down the leg. I stood beside the Colonel watching Dwyer but not paying much attention to what he was doing. Of a sudden something happened that made me doubt whether I was in my right senses. As I stood watching Dwyer swabbing the colt's off front leg that was white half way to the knee, it turned brown. I started to say something then checked myself. The Colonel and Dwyer never said a word. When Dwyer had finished with that leg he dried it with a towel, then started on the two white hind legs. In no time at all some sticky substance began to come off and the colt had two brown hind legs. Then Dwyer stood up, took his can and cotton, walked in front of the horse and stood looking at him. He turned to the Colonel and said, "Mr. John, it's yourself is a grand animal painter. There is no more illigant star on any horse in County Limerick than yourself has painted on this one. Then he removed the star. As he was drying the horse's forehead he said, "Albert, would you be going up to the end box and bringing the winner of this here North Jersey stake down to his own box. He'll rest better the night." I said nothing but went up to the tack room, found a halter shank, went to the end box and brought a beautiful brown colt down to his own box that looked as fresh as a daisy and as though he had never run a mile and a quarter. As I was leading him in the Colonel said, "Albert, find me a cab. I am going back to the Holland House to a particularly good dinner." Mr. Pendelton, Sir, if I may say so, Sir, Jim the porter and I had a right smart snack of dinner that night and a game of cribbage. Thank you, Sir.

CHAPTER XI.

Dr. James Robertson Earns a Velvet Cap

You may remember that during Colonel Weatherford's birthday party little Mary Sedgwick had proposed that Enid Ashley, Mary, the Colonel and I should foregather together on each anniversary of the Colonel's birthday. The Colonel had taken her at her word, and a year later we four were celebrating the event in the Colonel's library.

Our memories harkened back to a year ago when the Colonel had told us the story of the brush that hung over his mantel, and we would give him no peace until he had told us another tale. He went through the ceremony of lighting his pipe in a slow and meditative way as though trying to call back events of the long ago and when his pipe was burning to his liking he told this tale:

Heddingham was a small, down-at-the-heel, third-rate English city. The people there were too old or too poor, or too impotent to leave. Endless flocks of pinched brick houses showed "Furnished Rooms" and "To Let" signs. One window, cleaner than the rest, bore a sign, "James Robertson, M.D."

Two and twenty years before, a young medical graduate, brilliant, and of great promise, to whom Oxford had said cum laude, and for whom the faculty and fellow-students at medical school prophesied great things, had answered an advertisement of old Dr. Cruthers of Heddingham for a young assistant. Two years later the aged Doctor had traveled on, but the assistant remained.

Through necessity he had moved from the upper to the lower town where he lived in one narrow, meagre, room surrounded by all of his possessions; the implements of his trade; a dingy suit or two; a few shirts, now a bit frayed at the cuffs, and two or three sombre neckties which dangled listlessly from the gas fixture. There was little else except his books and pictures, for with the passing of time his wants had grown ever less.

To this tall, spare, over-sensitive Doctor, prematurely gray at forty-eight, the sicknesses of the world had proved overwhelming. In the beginning he had fought for the things men prized — a position, a name. But day and night those whom fortune had passed by had need of him. Each day he stayed on at his post bound him tighter to their tragedies. He was not of the temper to wrestle with his practice. He could not exact his fees from those to whom paying meant sacrifice.

The years passed on. He moved to the narrow house among the "To Let" signs. The other doctors of the town forgot him. He carried help down dingy streets and out on country downs. But through these dreary days and nights an unfathomable yet knowing Providence, recognizing that men may not live by work alone continued to nourish this man's one dominant interest, his deep-rooted love of the Chase. He had been bred and born to the sport for his forbears had hunted the fox time out of mind.

As a school boy, then at Oxford, and later at medical school, James Robertson was never known to miss a chance

of a day's hunting. Buried as he was in the slums of Heddingham, he still reveled in the pageantry of the Hunt.

On the walls of his room were pictures of such great Grand
National horses as *Cloister* and *Manifesto,* and affixed by
thumbtacks were faded magazine pictures of himself in
"silks" or "scarlet" on horses he well remembered.

In a corner of his closet tucked out of sight was a pair of
well-boned boots of a length and straightness of leg to have
aroused the envy of the entire riding personnel of the London Stock Exchange.

His scarlet, mufti and even a set of racing colors made for
him by an admiring younger sister, were carefully put away
in a disintegrating leather trunk.

His one and only recreation at Heddingham had been his
occasional days to hounds on foot and they had been very
occasional. The Heddingham side of the country was decidedly poor and was hunted as seldom as possible; just
enough to show some consideration to the owners of coverts
and a few subscribers in and about the town. Foxes were hard
to find and when found there was much galloping in flint-
strewn fields.

On hunting mornings the good Doctor would aim to be at
the Meet before hounds or horses arrived, for he enjoyed seeing the Hunt assemble. From some inconspicuous nook he
would appraise horses and riders as they came up. With the
exception of Jim Maltby, the job master, it is doubtful
whether any mounted person knew him, yet he had been one
of the straightest men to hounds in his part of England, and
those large, sensitive hands which now handled the surgeon's implements so deftly had once suggested things to
horses that gave them confidence and contentment.

During a day's sport he would stick relentlessly to the line for so long as it was possible for one on foot to maintain contact with hounds through sight or sound. On many occasions he would find himself long miles from home at the end of a cold winter afternoon but would trudge on towards Heddingham buoyed up, his mind aglow in reviewing each move of fox and hounds.

Why, on so many of the days on which he might have enjoyed this diversion, critical things should have happened to his people, was one of his perplexities. He would spend weeks in contemplation of a day's hunting from some fixture available to one afoot, and then have his plans come to naught. So often had this happened that he had finally become resigned.

On a raw, mist-soaked evening towards the end of January, the Doctor was returning from an outlying district. As he approached his room he noticed that an automobile had just pulled up in front of the house. Automobiles were very unusual on Tompkins Street. As he started up his steps a liveried chauffeur approached him and touching his cap, an act which gave the Doctor a queer quirk, said, "Please, Sir, are you Dr. Robertson?" "Yes," said the Doctor. "Oh, Sir, I'm very glad, Sir. I'm Lord Heddingham's man, Sir. We need a doctor very badly. Will you come to the Hall right away? The young master is took very bad, I'm told. His Lordship has 'phoned for Sir Henry Parrish to come down from London, but he can't get here for some hours, and we have been 'phoning to every doctor we could think of, but they are all out or away, and his Lordship sent me to town to bring any doctor I could find. Please come right away, Sir." Dr. Robertson entered the car. Heddingham Hall, Lord Heddingham, his landlord; the man who owned those miles and miles of squeezed brick houses; the Master of Fox-hounds. They said he owned 100,000 acres one place or an-other. The car sped on.

As they passed through the village of Eversham where the Doctor had spent the early evening sitting with old Mrs. Tabbs, he saw the light still burning in the bedroom, and knew that death was not many days away from that wee cot-tage. Just ahead the great towers of the Hall silhouetted against the sky. The iron gates of the park were open and the old lodge-keeper was in front of his cottage. He too knew that grave things were afoot.

As the car drew up at the Hall, the massive front door was opened, and some one approached. From seeing him in scarlet and velvet cap the Doctor recognized the Earl of Hedding-ham. "Is this the Doctor? I'm Lord Heddingham. It was good of you to come so promptly. Please come with me."

They climbed the great stairs. A feverish, pain-racked boy of twelve, heir to 100,000 acres of England, lay very ill that night in Heddingham Hall.

As he climbed the stairs the Doctor felt ill at ease in the vast majesty of the place. Twenty years of constant contact with poverty and poverty alone does this to one, but as he gazed on the patient he forgot Heddingham Hall.

When he had completed his examination, he directed searching questions to the attendant who had been with the boy during the day. They had gone abroad on a picnic in the pony cart. During the afternoon the boy complained of a severe pain. By the time they had reached home it had be-come very acute. Lord Heddingham and his lady were hunt-ing and were not expected home until late. A well-meaning nurse had diagnosed the complaint as an ordinary stomach ache and treated it accordingly. Had the boy ever complained of similar pains? Yes he had a number of times lately, but they seemed to pass off. The Doctor considered. The condition had been acute for seven hours. It was apparently the culmination of a condition of some duration. A month or more. "My Lord, I wish to speak with you." The anxious, distraught parents led him to an adjoining room. "My Lord, I counsel an immediate operation here and now. I fear the consequences of any delay. It may be three hours before Sir Henry arrives. I wish it were possible for you to reach your own local physician, but I understand he is not available."

Lord Heddingham was a man of the world and of affairs. He had served England at home and abroad and was a keen appraiser of men. Surely there was something very potent in the causes which lay back of this threadbare, worn suit, the frayed cuffs, and shabby shoes. Torn and distressed as he was, he cleared his mind.

"You come from Heddingham, Doctor?" "Yes, my Lord. I have practised there twenty-two years. I was Dr. Cruthers' assistant at the time of his death."

"You have performed this operation many times?" "A great many." "You consider the risk of awaiting Sir Henry's coming one that as parents, Lady Heddingham and I have no right to assume?" "I do." "Then I ask you to operate, Doctor. You will, I know, credit my recent questions regarding yourself to my intense anxiety."

Two hours later a greatly relieved Doctor sat watching the regular breathing of a pale little boy whose fair hair, shoved far back, showed a noble forehead. There was the semblance of a smile on the Doctor's thin gray face. He had had grave misgivings two hours before.

In the far corner of the room a mother and father brought closer together than they had been for years held each other's hands and waited for the boy to come out of the anaesthetic. As they sat thus they heard from afar the faint rumble of a car being driven at a great pace.

Sir Henry Parrish, tall, impressive, commanding, entered the room. He had been out at dinner when the message reached him and still wore his immaculate evening clothes.

The Doctors went into earnest conference. To the anxious parents it seemed as though they muttered together for endless hours, but when they had finished, England's great Doctor knew whatever could be known. He requested Lord and Lady Heddingham and Dr. Robertson to speak with him in the adjoining room.

Sir Henry strode over to the fireplace, put his hands behind his back, squared his powerful shoulders, looked straight and hard into Lord Heddingham's face, and said, "Lord Heddingham, what I say must be in the nature of conjecture and opinion, but I give it as my opinion that Dr. Robertson's courage, and I assure you it took a great deal, his prompt perception of the situation, and his skill exercised under very trying circumstances may for all we know have saved your son's life. One thing we do know and that is, that barring the unforeseen your son is comparatively speaking out of danger. I congratulate you both from the bottom of my heart, and it is a pleasure to felicitate a fellow practitioner on so fine a piece of work,"—and he strode over and shook Dr. James Robertson of Tompkins Street, Heddingham, by the hand, and Sir Henry's face glowed and every part of him glowed as he did so, for he was a great doctor and a great man, and it was naught to him that this country doctor was threadbare.

On a late Sunday afternoon a month hence, Dr. Robertson sat ruminating in his well-worn leather armchair. Heddingham was in the grip of a plague of influenza and he was sorely wearied mentally, physically and spiritually. After gazing into space for some time he re-read a letter from Hawk & Steinmetz, Collection Agency,

Dr. James Robertson,
45 Tompkins Street,
Heddingham.
Dear Sir:

Our clients, The Medical Publishing Co., have placed in our hands for immediate collection their account against you in the sum of Eleven Pounds, Eight Shillings and Nine Pence.

You have been under agreement to discharge this indebtedness on the basis of One Pound per week. In this our clients have been most generous. It is now three weeks since you have made any remittance.

In view of this default, our clients elect to consider now due the entire balance of Eleven Pounds, Eight Shillings and Nine Pence.

Unless this is paid at once we shall be forced to take such action for the protection of our clients as the situation may warrant.

Yours etc.

HAWK & STEINMETZ.

With a seeming effort he arose and went to his desk and busied himself for a long time in studying the intricacies of his check book. Now and again he would run his fingers through his gray-tinged hair and tattoo with his pen upon the edge of his desk. Then he drew a check for one pound and

wrote a letter. This accomplished he returned to his armchair and started to write.

The Earl of Heddingham
to
JAMES ROBERTSON, M.D.
Professional Services.

There he stopped. His foot tapped the floor. What would
seem fair and proper?

In twenty-odd years he had performed many such opera-
tions for nothing for those who could pay nothing. Sometimes
he had received two pounds. Once he remembered five
pounds. The foot went on tapping. There had been ten visits
to the Hall, but transportation had been furnished. Yet it was
a long way to the Hall. Say four shillings a visit — That
would be two pounds. Then for the operation. How about
ten pounds? That seemed fair enough — a total of twelve
pounds. And so the bill was made and sent.

The following Wednesday was the first of the month. As
he returned home from supper at the Dairy Restaurant after
an afternoon in the outlying districts, he noticed the usual
first of the month mail. How true it was, he thought with a
wry smile, that he never received mail except on the first of
the month. A year or more would roll by without his receiv-
ing a personal letter.

There was a bill from Jim Maltby for the hire of horse
and buggy. A note from his landlady, Mrs. Lemuel Tibbetts,
hoping that he would oblige with the rent as things were in-
tolerable bad. Small bills from his wash lady, news dealer,
chemist, and an extremely unpleasant letter from Hawk &

Steinmetz with the unpleasant tidings that they were sending a representative to call upon him. Then his mind wandered off to a contemplation of the uncanny way influenza had of slipping into pneumonia among his ill-nourished and poorly nursed people.

In search for relief he settled down to read. For a week or two he had been browsing through the Letters of John Keats and thoroughly enjoying them, but to a doctor there had been grave foreboding in the last two letters. He sensed what was coming and was rather inclined to close the book, yet read on and came to Keats' letter to his friend and confidant, Charles Brown, written when they were taking Keats to Rome to die; one of the most tragic utterances in all of our literature. It's a letter none but the buoyant should ever read.

James Robertson gently closed the book, ran his fingers through his hair, rested his arms on his knees, let his head rest in his hands, and thus he sat. "God," he murmured, "surely this can't be all there is to it; all there is to life! I can't leave these people. Some one must care for them, yet for some reason, I can't seem to manage things if I stay."

There was a knock at the door. Mrs. Tibbetts handed him a letter.

An hour or two later, Carlyle, as Whistler has portrayed him, looked down from his place above the desk upon a man with his head bent forward on his arms. In his one hand he still held a letter. If Carlyle could have seen under those folded arms, he would have seen a smile that might have stirred his rugged old heart. The letter ran thus:

Dear Dr. Robertson:

I may have difficulty in couching what I wish to say in

[184]

words which will give adequate expression to what is in my mind and heart, but I hope you will comprehend the distinction between charity and well earned reward.

I received your statement in the sum of twelve pounds.

Following your now so memorable first visit to us, Lady Heddingham and I concerned ourselves with learning something of your life and activities in Heddingham; not, I assure you, my dear Doctor, in the spirit of prying or idle curiosity, but rather with the desire of learning if possible something about one to whom we feel under such heavy obligation.

I think I may say that we now have a fairly comprehensive picture of the part you have played in this community, and we are not unmindful that much of that part has been enacted for the benefit of our tenantry.

I will not attempt to voice my feelings of admiration for the self-denial which prompts a man to give to others the most vital years of his life, and his all.

I send you herewith my check for one thousand pounds being the amount Sir Henry Parrish now informs me he would have charged, had he, rather than yourself, performed the operation,—and with it comes our most profound gratitude.

I now venture upon a proposal to which I sincerely hope you will accede.

Mr. Maltby, the job master, informs me that you are an ardent foxhunter, and have often been out with us on foot. He further tells me that you are a first-rate man across country.

I have today taken the liberty of sending a brown horse whom we call *Chancellor* to Mr. Maltby's stable with the necessary tack, clothing, etc., and I hope you will permit me to maintain the horse there for you during the balance of the season. He is a workmanlike horse that has carried both Lady Heddingham and myself. We hope we may see you out with us as often as hounds meet on your side of the country.

I wish, Doctor, that you would appreciate the fact that as the principal land-owner in this neighborhood, you have put me under very considerable obligations by your splendid work among the people, and that from my standpoint it is a privilege to be permitted to do something to counterbalance this obligation.

Lady Heddingham joins with me in expressions of regard, and our son is emphatic in his desire that you will look in upon him some time in passing. He is continually referring to your stirring stories that so softened his days of convalescence.

We should all be glad to see you at any time.

HEDDINGHAM.

There were some things that it would have been hard for Carlyle to understand. He would have been perplexed to have seen a man in the back room of 45 Tompkins Street very late that night dressed in a pair of beautifully fitting brown leather breeches, highly polished black boots, well burnished spurs, and contemplating those boots, breeches and spurs with eyes which gave a suggestion of moisture.

As Colonel Weatherford finished telling us the story he went over to his desk, opened a lower drawer, found an old copy of the English *Field,* opened it at a certain page and handed it to us. At the top of the page was a picture of a

Dr. Robertson of Heddingham.

tall, lightly built man, sitting his horse as only a born horseman can sit a horse. Underneath we read:

Dr. James Robertson, the popular Secretary of the Heddingham Hunt, riding his workmanlike hunter, *Chancellor*.
Dr. Robertson piloted Lord Heddingham's crack horse,
Bennington to a well earned victory in the Hunt Steeplechase
last month.

Dr. James Robertson was wearing a velvet cap.

CHAPTER XII.

An Evening in Mr. Keener's Barn

I HAD been in town for a week and as the New York Express slowed up at the station of that pleasant city on the Hudson which serves as the gateway to my hill country twenty miles inland, I happened to look out of the window and spied my old friend Alderman O'Toole.

With that nicety with which some things are arranged in this world it was ordained that I should disembark head on to the Alderman.

"Mr. Pendleton! If it wasn't yourself I was thinking about not once but a thousand times this very day," and drawing me aside out of hearing of my fellow travelers, he said in a good, hearty Irish whisper, "Be to Jim Keener's barn at eight o'clock tonight. It's a fine main of nine foights we're to have sure enough. O'Mara's bur-eds against young Drummond's. Nine bur-eds apiece, and it's O'Mara's Red Breasted Blacks their very selves, the darlings, he's going to foight. It will be a grand event altogether. And would you mind to say nothing of the occurrence to the lads over to your country for wasn't the carowd at the last foight so bad they like to suffocate the bur-eds to say nothing of attracting the State Pulice. It was the Chief of our City Pulice himself that had to tell Officer Melch to keep his motorcycle engine running wide open so as the State boys wouldn't hear the palaver what was going on in the barn."

At eight o'clock I was at the scene of battle, seated on one of a series of stout planks supported on five-gallon kegs. My principal regret was that I had had no opportunity to get word of the event to Colonel Weatherford.

We were indeed a distinguished audience. Both parties in local politics were well represented. The trotting horse contingent was out in full force. The wholesaler of White Horse Cellar Scotch was hobnobbing with the substantial citizen who performed the same function for Canadian Ale. Pierre Jabbat, who had the "exclusive" in our district for light wines, brandy and cordials, was affability itself. The gorgeous, high-powered, mauve upholstered cars of these three gentlemen were parked in Mr. Keener's back meadow side by side with the small drab models of the local bankers. On a front bench two of our "smartest" lawyers were swapping stories with old Doctor Tate and Judge Glendenning. We were all there.

I had just consulted my watch and found it to be ten minutes past eight when there was a movement and bustle over by the door and a man back of me said to his neighbor, "Here comes the old man." And the next moment Colonel Weatherford, looming well over the heads of those around him, came in search of a seat. By that time the barn was packed. Then I heard Mr. Keener's jovial voice saying, "Just a minute, Colonel, just a minute, and I'll fix you up on the chopping block" — a threat the Colonel took in good part. In jig time Mr. Keener and his son Joe brought the block down front. As he was taking his seat the Colonel caught my eye and waved a salutation. As he sat down the man behind me said, "There's a back for you."

Of the main held that night in Keener's barn the less said the better. A more disagreeable and miserable performance was never held in our county. Had I been able to squeeze my way out I should have left the place long before the end.

Fred Drummond was a young sporting farmer living a few miles north of me, who raised a few well-bred colts every year which he broke, schooled and hunted himself. He was an invaluable friend to the Hunt, a splendid farmer, and a great favorite with us all.

He had recently become interested in game birds, but as yet knew very little about this intricate and elevating pursuit. In an ill-starred moment he had issued a challenge to Tom O'Mara.

A word about Tom O'Mara. It seems the destiny and fate of all neighborhoods to suffer under the blight and tyranny of at least one major bully. I remember once discussing O'Mara with Colonel Weatherford and he said, "Pendleton, a person like O'Mara is a necessity to every district. He serves as a mirror in which the bully in each of us is reflected. The sight and contemplation of him is a healthy deterrent."

O'Mara was an exceedingly well-known character who had acquired a substantial fortune one way or another. He wielded a certain political power, was the owner of a well-known hotel, the silent partner in a successful contracting firm which was never forgotten by the powers that be when patronage was being handed about, and he called more than one of the owners of the shiny cars by their first names. In addition to all this he knew more about game chickens and the breeding, conditioning and fighting of them than any man for two hundred miles around.

I will dispose of the battle in the fewest possible words.

Fred Drummond's first cock had not been in the pit more than half a minute before it was evident that his birds had no right to be pitted against O'Mara's.

Fred swallowed hard and took his punishment until he had lost his third bird. Then he stood up and made certain statements and confessions that were not easy for a young farmer to make in the face of that particular audience.

He said he now recognized that his country birds were not up to fighting Mr. O'Mara's fine cocks. That he was very sorry to have brought so many people there and not to be able to show better sport, and then asked O'Mara if he would mind if he withdrew the other six birds and forfeited the match that way as those were the only birds he had, and he didn't think the people there would enjoy seeing birds killed that didn't really have any chance, and that the next time he fought he would sure try and put up a better match.

The audience took it all good naturedly and seemed only too glad to have the affair ended.

Not so Tom O'Mara. It was evident that he had been drinking heavily and was in a very ugly mood in consequence. He was a monstrous fellow. I don't know whether they make such a thing as a size twenty collar but if they do O'Mara must wear one. He stood up and told the world at large what he thought of Fred's birds and Fred himself and assured us that what Fred was getting was what any of us might expect to get if we went issuing challenges to his "Red Breasted Blacks," and that the thing would be a good lesson to some young upstarts that thought they knew something about fighting chickens.

Then he regaled us with the gastronomic pleasantry that his birds needed a bit of blood and he meant 'em to have it.

He said he knew what was going to happen before the main started and that's why he framed the conditions as he did, and that if Fred wanted to withdraw his birds why he could cough up $100 apiece, and so on. Then he thundered to Fred to bring on what remained of his grandmother's broody hens, and he'd give 'em something to worry about. He ended, "As long as I'm on my feet I want to say that I'll fight and lick any bird up to an ostrich. I don't care what it is, where it comes from, or who owns it. You all know my address." Then he sat down.

I looked over at Colonel Weatherford. I could only see his back, but there was something about the tilt of his head, the angle of his neck, the pitch of his shoulders, that told me what was going on inside of him. Twice I saw him start to rise, then change his mind. He was evidently biding his time. When the wretched affair was finally over he rose to his feet. The hubbub subsided and he adressed himself to O'Mara.

"Mr. O'Mara," he said, "you have the most perfect fighting birds I have seen for many years, and I compliment you, Sir, on the splendid condition in which you brought them to this contest.

"I was very much interested in your statement that you would fight them against any bird up to an ostrich in size. Just what did you mean, Sir?"

O'Mara was exceedingly pleased by the compliments, for the Colonel was considered a great authority upon all matters of sport and was popular among all ranks of people.

He stood up and said he meant just what he said. "Of course, Colonel," he continued, "I don't mean to say that my birds maybe could kill a bird that was too much too big for 'em, but I reckon that no bird bigger or smaller could kill

[193]

my birds. You might find some kind of a big bird, but when you found him he wouldn't fight in a pit. As a matter of fact I never heard of any kind of a bird that would kill a good game chicken in a pit, and if there is he can't kill mine and if there's anybody thinks they can it's going to cost 'em money to think so."

Then I became suspicious. The Colonel's voice assumed a tone I had learned to beware of. It became soft and conciliatory. "Well, Mr. O'Mara, that's very interesting, very interesting. Those are certainly wonderful birds of yours, but our friends haven't had much sport here tonight, have they?"

"That they haven't," said O'Mara. "Rotten night I call it. A lot of yellow-livered trash those birds of Drummond's."

"Well," continued the Colonel, "of course, you know a lot more about this sport than I do, but I was wondering if I might not accept your challenge on the following terms. Before I proceed I wonder if I could ask Mr. Pendleton, whom I see in the audience, if he would write this down so that we would have a record of it.

"Now, then, I will match one bird of some species, kind or classification of my own selection against one so-called game cock to be selected by you for — what shall we say; I know you have little interest in small stakes. Might we say $500? If by any chance my bird should defeat yours, not, I presume, a likely contingency, then we are to continue the match until my bird is disposed of or a total of thirteen of your birds shall have been defeated, whichever event shall happen first. Perhaps we might say that we will fight each bird after the first, at $250 a bird. I shall be ready sixty days from tonight at the same time and place."

I think I said before that O'Mara had dined well. He was

genuinely confused in respect to certain details, but was too arrogant to admit it. "All right, Colonel," he said. "It suits me. Your bird and your pocketbook are in for a fine trimming."

"I suggest," said the Colonel, "that we ask Alderman O'Toole to hold the stakes. Five hundred dollars of the Colonel's crisp new bills took what looked to me a very perilous journey from hand to hand until they came to rest in the Alderman's ample palm. O'Mara did the same.

By this time I had made a legible copy of the terms of the main which went the way of the stake and was deposited in Mr. O'Toole's fat black wallet; and Mr. Keener's guests went home.

The next morning I could not resist walking across my lower meadow to the Colonel's to talk over the night's events and to learn of his plans. It didn't take me more than a minute to discover that the Colonel had no desire or intention of discussing the matter. He acted as though he wished to forget the whole business just as soon as possible. I took the hint and never referred to the subject again.

I have a calendar on which I note coming events and I marked the date of this match with a large circle and let it go at that, but on many occasions during the next two months my mind reverted to the scene in Keener's barn. Poor Fred Drummond with his flushed face and distressed looks. O'Mara's sneering, bullying voice. The Colonel's suave manner and innocent sounding words, and the odd terms of the match.

The Colonel and I rode together, hunted together, dined together, and spent many an evening around his library fire, but never a single reference was made to the coming event.

Thursday, the 16th, had been the night fixed upon, and on the morning of that day I went over to the Colonel's, for frankly there was such complete silence that I was almost beginning to wonder whether the match might not have been abandoned. To my surprise I was informed that the Colonel was away from home, and that his man, Albert, had gone with him.

At noon-time I was on the verge of calling up my friend, the Alderman, for news of the event, when I was told that Long Distance wanted me on the telephone. Central said New Haven was calling and presently a voice said, "Mr. Pendleton, this is Professor Foster of New Haven. I'm speaking for Colonel Weatherford, who wishes me to remind you of the School Meeting at Mr. Keener's house this evening." I thanked him and rang off. Professor Foster at New Haven. A fine how-do-you-do I thought. But at least the thing was on.

A quarter before eight o'clock that evening again saw me in Mr. Keener's barn and if not on the same plank and supported by the same little kegs,— then ones very much like them.

I was decidedly nervous. I knew that the money at stake was but a drop in a bucket to the Colonel, but the entire business had a bizarre flavor which I did not relish. As I now viewed the matter I could not understand why and how Weatherford, of all people, could have permitted himself to become embroiled in such a situation. Nothing was further from his taste and character. Of course a person like O'Mara riled Weatherford, who was at heart a good deal of a knight errant. O'Mara's treatment of young Drummond had incensed him and he could not reconcile himself to a condition of affairs which permitted a savage like O'Mara to ride "high, wide and fancy." This was all very well, but I contemplated with misgivings how the Colonel would feel were O'Mara put in a position to crow over him and patronize him.

At eight o'clock O'Mara came in followed by his colored handler. I saw O'Mara look at his watch and I wished the Colonel would arrive and get the thing over with. Then he entered followed by a small, elderly man with a gray beard, a few wisps of gray hair on the top of his head, and wire-rimmed spectacles worn at a very crooked angle. The little man seemed tremendously interested in all he saw, and was no sooner seated than he extracted a notebook, and, giving his spectacles an impatient pull, commenced to write. The Colonel's inseparable servant, Albert, was of the party; he carried a box covered with a dark cloth. What a continuity of purpose, to clothe one's face with an expression of impersonality when one is young and wear it to the grave as Albert did! There was Albert carrying that ominous looking box into the center of Keener's barn with the same impersonal expression with which I had seen him waiting on the Colonel time out of mind.

But I will get on with this indescribable main. I may see many more affairs between birds but never, I hope, one like this.

The appointed hour had arrived. O'Mara's colored handler commonly known as "Cocoanut," a great burly, slouching fellow, but a past master of the science, stepped over the two foot wall and entered the pit. He had one of O'Mara's magnificent gladiators, a bird walked and conditioned to the last word, tucked under his arm. Judge Dwyer, so called from having officiated so many years at our trotting races, who had been appointed referee for the main, followed him. The Judge turned to Colonel Weatherford and said, "Are you ready, Colonel?" Upon which the Colonel said, "Quite ready, Judge."

At these words the imperturbable Albert removed the cover from his box and with extreme caution extracted a bird the like of which I warrant was never seen in the world before. A bird sinister and uncanny. Whatever its natural color may have been it now rivaled a bird of paradise. It had been painstakingly plucked and trimmed beyond recognition, and the remaining feathers dyed or painted every shade and color of the spectrum. It's great hooked beak was daubed a strong purple. The wings which gave the impression of being exceptionally large were unclipped but partly secured to its side by a contrivance of which broad bands of adhesive tape played a major part.

With a face upon which there was no semblance of expression and with all the little niceties and formalities with which he would have presented a ruddy canvasback duck for the Colonel's inspection and approval, Albert first exhibited the bird-apparition to the Colonel and then, tucking the bird under his arm in the most approved fashion, stepped into the pit.

While Albert had been bowing and showing the bird to the Colonel, the little gray man had given his glasses a particularly impetuous tug, stood up, leaned over the bird, peered at him, consulted his watch, and as his pen began to fly across the paper I heard him mutter, "8:14 p.m. Eyes same as reference in 3 p. above."

The audience proceeded to get out of hand. Those in the front row crowded forward and hung over the pit. Those in the rear climbed on the benches. This not sufficing they

The pit in Mr. Keener's barn.

climbed from bench to bench until they were all milling, barging and jostling each other. Mr. Keener and those in authority were at their wits' end. The stout little wooden kegs which at best were only filling in the off season between "apple" crops, went rolling and spinning about.

O'Mara's reaction was one of alarm, and I saw him twice start to his feet, but from his expression I knew he was muddled in his mind and at a loss to know what tack to take.

Cocoanut's eyes were revolving about in seas of white. His mouth was open and his lower lip was sagging. He looked at Albert — at Albert's bird — then at O'Mara. Finding no comfort or support he automatically bound the steel gaffs to his bird's spurs, winding the soft leather lashings in a slow, deliberate manner as though playing for time. He slowly extracted his scissors from his hip pocket, appeared to toy with them, and stood glaring at the bird under Albert's arm. Then with evident misgivings he clipped his bird's wings. I heard the Colonel say to the referee, "Judge, I elect to fight my bird without gaffs," and the Judge say, "As you wish, Colonel." The Judge looked at Cocoanut and Cocoanut nodded, then Albert nodded, the two birds were put and held down eight feet apart on their respective lines, and the audience sat down to see what they would see.

There could have been no worms boring in the century-old hand-hewn beams above us or we must surely have heard them — so still was it in the barn. Then I heard Judge Dwyer snap out the word, "Foight," and the birds were released.

We waited expectantly for the whir of wings and feathers and the flash of color as the birds attacked. It was not to be. This was to be no ordinary fight. Some deep-lying instinct of self-preservation appeared to be warning O'Mara's fine cock.

He strutted, challenged, bullied, threatened and blustered, but did not strike.

The Colonel's bird of mystery stood where and as Albert had left him. He had not moved a fraction of an inch. Once he languidly shifted his weight from one leg to another. He affected the attitude of a ne'er-do-well country rake slouching by a country "pub." As well as we could judge he never so much as noticed O'Mara's bird. He was plainly bored, irritated and annoyed by the entire performance. His adversary, however, could withstand the urge of battle no longer. He had been working himself up to a blind rage. There was a flash and he had assailed the Colonel's challenger. It was only then that the Colonel's bird seemed to notice the other and with uncanny dexterity he avoided the assault.

The crowd started to grow restless. Some one hissed. Others followed suit. Then O'Mara rose to his feet and in a very disagreeable voice said, "Colonel, is this some d—— hoax you are trying to play? Well let me tell you it's going to be no hoax about the money as you will find out and I serve notice on Alderman O'Toole to that effect right now. It don't make so much difference to me, 'cause I get the dough, but I don't like the idea of all my friends coming away out here on no practical joke. Your bird ain't got any fight in him and you know it. He's just going to sulk till my bird kills him but these gents don't want to sit here looking at murder."

The Colonel made no response. It was now evident that O'Mara's bird was determined on action,— final action. He started. There was a vicious swirl and the drumming of wings. Then something happened that is hard to depict in words. It is impossible for the human eye to follow all the movements of a fighting bird but my eyes were glued on what was going on and I saw as well as any one what happened. I saw the Colonel's atrocious looking bird standing as though about to yawn with boredom. In my ears were the hisses of those around me. Then I saw O'Mara's bird in the air and driving towards his victim. Then, something that moved so quickly and silently that it seemed more like a shadow than anything tangible, shot out from Weatherford's bird and instantaneously I saw the neck of O'Mara's fine bird held in a great scrawny yellow claw. I had no sooner digested this phenomenon than I saw the claw and the head of the cock being slowly drawn towards a long, curved, purple beak. Then I saw the beak open and the head of the cock disappear. Then there was something resembling an impatient jerk or wrench and the headless remains of Boss Thomas Nevin O'Mara's best bird were tossed languidly across the pit.

You could have heard a pin drop. It wasn't just a pause of surprise. It continued. It hung heavy. There was but one sound. The flying pen of the little gray man racing across the page of his notebook. Colonel Weatherford reached for his pipe, but beyond this there seemed no movement around me.

Then the silence was broken, and it was completely broken. A great towering, raging, purple-faced man was on his feet. Never have I heard such an avalanche of abuse. He roared that he was through. He withdrew the rest of his birds. This was the worst piece of malicious crookedness in the history of the game. Then followed a categorical list of the things he would do.

When he had exhausted himself the Colonel arose and in a voice that left not the slightest doubt in any one's mind what he wanted and what he was going to get said, "I will ask Alderman O'Toole kindly to read the written terms and conditions of this main. I will ask him to read slowly and distinctly. I want every man in this building to hear each and every word."

The Alderman read the terms of the main.

"Now," said Colonel Weatherford turning full upon O'Mara and shooting out his arm and forefinger at him, "I have the right to demand of you that you put twelve more birds one after another into that pit. Following the twelfth bird you will owe me $3000 in addition to the $500 deposited with the Alderman. If I want those birds put into that pit I will have them put in and all of them.

"Now, O'Mara, if you know what's good for you, you will listen to me. I came here two months ago tonight and saw a brutal performance. Not by your birds but by you. It is solely because of what you did to my neighbor, Fred Drummond, that I am here tonight. This whole affair is repugnant to me in the extreme. I say with candor that to have anything whatever to do with you irritates me beyond measure. I consider you an institution this neighborhood has to tolerate in spite of itself. Now this is what I'm prepared to do and this only. Mind you I have no intention of arguing the matter with you.

"I will release you from the $3000.

"I will direct Alderman O'Toole to turn over the $1000 he is holding, $500 of mine and $500 of yours, to some worthy charity or cause of his own selection, and you will forthwith deliver six of the remaining birds to my young friend, Fred Drummond. I will give you one minute to accept this. If you do not accept I will demand your next bird."

I think the only thing I enjoyed during that night was the look on Fred Drummond's face as he put six very choice "Red Breasted Black" game cocks into the back of his car.

When we were out in the open, Colonel Weatherford said, "Pendleton, I want you to know Professor Foster of New Haven, one of the foremost ornithologists. As you probably know, he is our greatest authority on the American eagle. He has been making some observations this evening on the bald-headed variety."

CHAPTER XIII.

St. Margaret of Ives

He arrived with his horse on Thursday. On Saturday the manager of the riding academy received word that the Polish officer had been taken ill. Three days later he answered his final roll call.

I never saw him, but they said that the two nurses who attended him at the hospital knelt at the bedside when it was all over, and wept, and that the surgeon told an associate going down in the elevator that the young Polish officer was the most engaging personality he had ever encountered.

The hospital, not knowing what else to do, communicated with the Polish Consulate from whence a supercilious and indifferent young man arrived to give directions and take charge of the personal effects. From the hospital the bored young diplomat proceeded to a scanty room in a meagre boarding house in Brooklyn. What it was he discovered there I never learned, but the young man came out of the lodging house at double quick time, headed for the nearest telephone, called up his superior who, in turn, started the wires humming to Washington and the cables humming to Poland, and within the hour two very elderly and dignified persons arrived to take charge. That's all I know of the matter.

A week later Tom Murdock took time from his law practice to write me as follows:

[205]

Dear Pendleton:

There is the sweetest blood mare I have ever set my eyes on for sale at the Academy. I understand she belonged to some foreign officer who died, or something, so they must get rid of her. $500 will do the trick. Why don't you run down and see her? She is just your kind.

Hastily,

TOM MURDOCK.

I ran down, rode and jumped the mare, became more en-amoured than I have ever been of any horse before or since, and bought her. As I entered my taxi after completing the transaction I remembered that I had failed to ascertain the mare's name, so I went back and asked the manager. He consulted his book and said, "*St. Margaret of Ives.*" She arrived at my farm on May 25th. On the 26th I started by motor to meet Colonel Weatherford at his Canadian salmon water.

I was clipping off the miles through the Province of Quebec when at about four o'clock in the afternoon I came to a sizeable town. There had been a shower a few minutes before, making the streets slippery and in avoiding a small boy with a bundle of afternoon newspapers under one arm, the rear wheel of my car hit a culvert and something let go. The sympathetic garage man said it would take two days — perhaps three — to procure the necessary parts from Montreal.

As we talked a passer-by stopped to look at the damaged car. Turning, I recognized him at once. I would have known him among ten million. Twenty-six years ago he had attended a convention as a delegate from the McGill chapter of my fraternity, and we had seen much of one another. He had come over from England to Canada, where his people had important holdings, and entered the Canadian university, planning to settle in the country after graduation.

Of course I recognized him, for I had been more impressed and influenced by him than by any fellow student I had ever met. He was a famous athlete — a fine sportsman, and above all, a born leader though of a quiet, retiring disposition. I gleaned some lessons from his book, and gleaned them so thoroughly that his precepts had become a very part of me, and there he was standing looking at my wrecked car.

I called him by name, stepped forward and held out my hand. He had no idea who I was, but his face lit up with the gay spontaneous smile I remembered so well. When I re-called our meeting years ago a tinge of pain came over his face — pain that he should have forgotten even a casual ac-quaintance and he carried me off to his home to stay until my car could be repaired. It was a spacious, generous brick house set in a landscaped park, for he was the man of affairs in that district. He had lived up to the promise of his youth.

At tea time we were joined by his wife, a courtly, yet cor-dial and gracious woman. At dinner I was presented to the daughter, Margaret, a tall fair-haired girl of twenty-two, just returned from a long stay abroad. She was a striking girl and as father and daughter stood together with their backs to the fireplace waiting for dinner to be announced I thought them the handsomest pair I had seen in many years. After dinner my host and hostess were under the necessity of at-tending some local meeting, and the daughter and I were to entertain one another pending their return.

There was a twang in the air of that far north country even in May so we pulled our chairs up to the open grate in which great chunks of cannel coal were burning. It is not always easy for youth and middle age to converse together throughout an evening, yet on this evening I lamented the too quick passage of time. She had much of her father's ardor and enthusiasm — his love of sport, fair play and tolerance, but above all, a deep Catholic sympathy for all who were oppressed.

During two intensive years she had been seeing Europe under auspices which only strong diplomatic connections can make possible. She returned confounded by the century-old hates of neighboring peoples and her sympathy aflame for those who lived under alien yokes — the Poles and all others whose heritage had been sold or bartered away.

We finally drifted into a discussion of military equitation as practiced in the different armies and she had just finished a vivid and telling description of a memorable gathering of cavalry officers of many nations and the magnificent riding of each, when the thought struck me that I should get a telegram through to Colonel Weatherford. In the excitement of the afternoon I had never ascertained even the name of the town I was staying in, so I asked her. "This is Ives," she said.

She was sitting on a low bench with her back to the fire, but her head turned toward the fireplace. I don't know whether I spoke to her or was only reflecting aloud, but I said, half to myself, *"St. Margaret of Ives."* I was not looking at her when I said this, yet sensed that she made a quick movement. When I looked up she was staring at me with wide open eyes and quite plainly grasping the side of the bench with her hands. My remark seemed innocent enough to me, yet I could only conclude that she had resented my seeming familiarity. I arose, went to a nearby table for a match for my pipe and thinking to make amends, said, "You know, I have just acquired a little bay mare called *St. Margaret of Ives.*"

As I mentioned, I was standing up and lighting my pipe when I said this. The next thing I knew she was standing in front of me. "You — you own her —" she said, and there was a tenseness in her voice nothing short of alarming. "How could you have her? You couldn't. It can't be the same one. Quick! Tell me about her." As she spoke she kept coming closer and closer to me, until she finally took hold of one of the buttons of my coat and twisted it nervously, while her great, inquiring eyes searched deeply into me. I told her the little that I knew.

She was of magnificent courage. There was no display of what was going on within her. She asked me if I minded being alone, said "good-night," turned and walked toward the door. Then she stopped, stood a moment, came back to me, took the lapels of my coat in her hands and said, "Are you fond of her?" "Yes," I said, "very fond." "Do you intend to keep her always?" "Always," I answered. "Thank you," she said, and left me. I never saw her again. Within the year the Convent of St. Cecilia received a novitiate.

The fall of that year came. I am grateful for the gift of memory which keeps forever green the myriad of happy characteristics of horses and dogs who meant much to me and grew old in my companionship. Of all my cherished memories of sport there is none more companionable than the autumn-tinted picture of the one and only one hunting season little *St. Margaret of Ives* and I ever had together. My mind never reverts to foxhunting of long ago but I see the little mare with her bewitchingly beautiful head and ingratiating ways. I contemplate even now the way she had of playing with her bit as she stepped so airily and lightly along; her intense way of turning her head whenever a hound opened and concentrating her entire being on the sound; then when naught would come of it, turning her head away with what always sounded to me like a monstrous sigh; her teasing to go always a trifle faster, yet never taking hold of her bit; her willingness to creep to her fences when creeping was necessary and her boldness in standing away and flying them when the going was good. I was for ever amused at her pressing desire to get to hounds by the most direct route and her intolerance of my more conventional way. I am told that there are people whose ears are deaf to the music of horses' feet in new fallen oak leaves — big, crisp, crinkly leaves — people unable to distinguish the gay rustling of thoroughbred feet from the dull listless thud of big-footed half-bred Irishmen. Why, *St. Margaret's* feet played a veritable autumn symphony through the leaves.

Thanksgiving day finally arrived, a day that marked the high point of achievement of all time for our hounds and foxes. The day's events have become a legend. At 4:30 in the afternoon, when not above three-quarters of an hour of day light was left, and after two hours and fifty-five minutes of running, only six from a field of seventy remained with hounds. At a quarter to five only Enid Ashley, Colonel Weatherford and I labored up the western slope of Pugsley Hill. At the summit Enid's *Jack Knife* and the Colonel's *Matchmaker* stopped and I went down the western slope alone with hounds.

It is all very well for people to say that I never should have done it but they who criticise never felt that bay mare under them. She was a law unto herself. She started down that long, far reaching hill with such buoyancy and supreme courage that I thought we were invulnerable. She instilled me with such exhilaration that day I became as another person. Then, it let go. I jumped off. I knew what it was. No tendon on earth could indefinitely support so high and valiant a courage.

I stood beside her with my hand resting on her wither and together we watched hounds race on toward the setting sun. Down through all the years I can see those small, sensitive, alert ears and great dark eyes following the fading hounds. When the final gleam of color sank below the peak of Stillings Mountain the sun had set for the last time for *St. Margaret of Ives* afield. I led her away.

Last Thursday a car came to a sudden stop in front of my driveway. I saw the occupant of the car studying my name on the letter box, then he looked toward the house and turned the car into the driveway. There he was, tall, erect, and now very gray. Motoring back from New York to Canada he was taking a detour toward the Berkshires and had seen my name on the mail box.

We sat together on the terrace through the hours of that so exquisite May afternoon talking of this and that, but I knew only too well that I conjured up an ancient wound that time could only partially heal.

As we talked, an old mare came around the corner of the house and went to cropping the rich grass under the apple trees. At each breath of air blossoms drifted down and nestled a while in the old matron's mane. "Is she meant to be loose about the lawn like that?" he asked. "Yes," I said. "Ah, an old favorite, I suppose." "Yes," I replied, "She is twenty-seven years old. I crippled her on a Thanksgiving Day

[211]

twenty-one years ago." "What do you call her?" he asked. I hesitated, then pretended that I had not heard him and we talked of other things.

CHAPTER XIV.

The Crest of Athelling Hill

I STRETCHED my muddy hunting boots to the library fire and leaned back in Colonel Weatherford's massive leather chair set upon enjoying one of those tingling late afternoon hours that come only to those who have spent the day afield. The Colonel rang for tea, pulled his chair close to the fire and we sat together in mellow yet uncommunicative companionship.

It had been a gray, sombering afternoon out on those big hills of ours. For hour upon hour a snarling, unrelenting wind had hurried leaden clouds across a leaden sky; a day for foxes to lay close; a day when the very thought of one's own reflection sobered one. Nature had seemed to be battling against all forms of life as though life were no concern of hers and every living thing sensed it and sought the companionship of its kind.

I finally found myself speculating as to whether sportsmen who spent much time afield were not prone to belittle the need of social and family ties and place over reliance on the friendliness of nature. Perhaps bachelors who have crossed the half-way mark occasionally feel this way on drear late afternoons. I wondered whether Colonel Weatherford had ever been assailed by such thoughts and looked over at him. To my surprise he was sitting bolt upright in his chair and gazing intently at a newly arrived English magazine. There was an expression on his rugged face I had never thought to see there. The usual mask of reserve had vanished and in its stead there was a note of sadness and longing. Resting the magazine on his lap he gazed into the fire a moment or two and then, as though reading my thoughts, said, "Pendleton, I don't suppose any of us are quite sufficient unto ourselves and certainly a snarling foxhunting day like this suggests that nature is not always a kindly, sympathetic playfellow. Loneliness is a common heritage." He picked up the magazine again, looked long and intently at whatever had so engrossed him and continued, "My thoughts have been very far away during the last few minutes for I have just re-lived the most memorable day of my life. It was a day to hounds." He settled back in his chair, again rested the magazine on his knees and went on:

Forty years ago, in the days when old George Trevelyn was Master, I was hunting down in Pennsylvania. One Saturday morning toward the end of October we met at a fixture known as the Dutch Minister's School House and were about to move on to our first covert when a girl whom no one seemed to know arrived at the Meet. She asked for Trevelyn and seemed distressed at finding he was not hunting. We were rather agog about her for she was turned out as only one woman in a million can turn themselves out for the field, and was mounted on a small, clean-bred brown mare of exquisite quality with her mane painstakingly braided. In those days very few women rode blood horses.

Hounds found almost immediately, fairly crashed out of covert and went away. I was riding a thoroughbred horse called *Gay Minstrel* by *St. Gatien,* the best conveyance across a big country I have ever owned or ridden; the sort you confidently ask to do things you would not attempt on the average horse. I was young and as hard as nails, and so settled down to ride and enjoy the sport to the full. In the turmoil of getting well away I entirely forgot our unknown visitor.

It was soon evident that we had unkenneled a good fox and had found him well for he ran a surprisingly straight and purposeful line.

The Dutch Minister's School House lay close to our northern boundary and we had planned to draw and hunt towards home. The fox planned otherwise. At the end of twenty minutes, in view of the pace and straightness of our line, we had slipped quite out of our country and were feeling our way through the vastness of the state of Pennsylvania. Riding a straight line became more and more difficult yet there was no abatement in the speed hounds were running. The field melted away not so much from the pace, for they were exceptionally mounted, but the fences were terrific, and in trying to avoid unjumpable places we were forever getting into farmyards or orchard lots from which there seemed no forward way out. Whenever during this scramble I looked back, the girl on the little brown mare was right in my "pocket" and I had navigated some rasping big fences.

I finally galloped down into a stretch of bottom land that I had never seen before. In front of me I saw a line of willows and then beyond them a dark stream far too wide to jump and on the far side, three feet from the bank, rose a five-board fence. It must be jumped or jumped at from the bottom of the unknown stream. I pulled up. Behind me I heard the others turn away and disappear. But hounds were running.

I brought my horse down to a walk, took hold of his head,

stepped him into the stream and started him for the fence. He refused. I turned him around. Hounds were streaming on. The music was faint now. I must be with them. I would ride at that fence for a fall. I heard the stamp of a horse's hoof. There stood the girl on the brown mare. "Go back," I called. She started for the fence. "Hold hard," I bellowed. As she passed me she smiled.

That little mare went down to the branch with her head loose, her ears forward, and her great dark eyes on what was in front of her. She landed in the water, took one stride and jumped for it.

(The Colonel took a breath. Then he leaned forward and tapped me on the knee.) In fifty years I have seen many horses hit many fences but never anything comparable to that. I'm not exaggerating when I say that from directly back of them where I stood the mare's legs appeared to be straight out to the off side, giving the impression of a horse lying on its side in the air. There was nothing between the girl and the ground and I expected to see her pinned to the earth. I kicked my feet out of the stirrups preparatory to running to her assistance, but by some mysterious means the mare worked her near front foot around and connected it with the ground. She then pitched forward on her head with such force that the reins were jerked out of the girl's hands, but the blood of *Eclipse* fought on. The mare made a desperate scramble; gained her feet; pitched forward a second time, recovered, and was up and sailing on. I saw the girl gather her reins, stop the mare, pat her, and look back at me. I went at the fence with what little heart I had left, leaving the task to *Gay Minstrel*. As he landed in the stream with a great, bold stride, the water sprayed over us and I loved the horse for

[216]

his high courage. He gathered himself and jumped, but as he took off I felt his hind feet slip and knew the unseen bottom had been treacherous to him. He cleared the fence in front but hit it a smashing blow behind and landed sprawling. A terrific lunge forward brought him up on his feet only to again pitch him on his head, but he was indomitable and refused to fall. When we finally recovered ourselves I had been astride every part of him from his ears to the root of his tail.

Upon rejoining my lone companion the smile I had been noticing was gone. She had an odd little way of quizzically puckering up her forehead suggestive of concern, and she now looked searchingly at me. "You should not have done it," I said. "But you led on," she answered. It was the first time I had heard her voice. As we galloped on in quest of hounds she was, indeed, one for a man to conjure about for from the beautifully-ironed silk hat to the barbarous Mother Hubbard riding skirt of that era, the picture was perfect; I was at an impressionable age.

That fox ran two hours and thirty-five minutes and we had it alone. Never have I worked as I did that day to stay with hounds, and no horse I ever owned could have lived with *Gay Minstrel* that afternoon and gone the route; yet the little French mare pressed him to the very end. I have never seen a woman's hunter comparable to her.

There is a great difference between an old hunting country and one that has never been ridden over. If an unjumpable brook didn't stop us it would be a swamp. If we circumvented the swamp there would be a monstrous fence with a drop on to a country road or something equally trying. We had in-and-outs over farm lanes that were never intended to be jumped. If hounds checked we still had to keep galloping to get to them. There was little chance to breathe our horses.

During all that memorable journey I never heard the mare lay a toe to a thing except the big fence. As we rattled along over fence and fence, I would look back to see them come over after every fence further complicated my feelings. It is seldom one ever sees a horse and rider so perfectly attuned to each other.

We at last climbed to a high upland country to which my memory often reverts. It was a scantily populated area of vast enclosures with pleasant, old fashioned post-and-rail fences, and we galloped together mile after mile over well-nigh perfect turf, meeting little covert and no plow.

Towards the end a fresh wind sprang up and blew the scent about. This came as a godsend to our tired horses, for on the high, windswept knolls hounds would be brought to their noses to work out the line.

For some miles a heavily wooded ridge had been looming up ahead of us, for which our fox was evidently making. I knew that if hounds once entered so vast a tract of woods we would never get them out, and felt that I should try and stop them. They were not my hounds, even though I had been thinking and acting otherwise for the last two hours.

Of a sudden hounds burst into a new and clamorous cry. *Gay Minstrel's* head and ears came up, and I felt a tautness under the saddle. Then my arm was clutched. "Look! Look!" the girl said. I looked, and ahead of us hounds were running their sinking fox from view.

We killed under the leafless branches of a dead oak tree standing as a beacon for all the country round; an ancient hoary giant which had probably guided our fox on his last valiant run for the covert.

[218]

After removing the mask and brush I turned to my companion to make the presentation. She was standing with her back to hounds, and her silk hat dangling from its cord. The mare stood near by with the reins over the pommel.

When I came with the trophies she turned away and said, "Please don't. Why must our glorious adventure have such an ending," and walked on down the slope with the mare following her. She was squeezing a small, crumpled handkerchief in her hand.

Turning to the hounds, I threw them the mask, put the brush in my pocket and led *Gay Minstrel* down to where she was sitting on a boulder; we sat together looking off over countless miles of rolling country to where our horizon met the sky. Below us a group of white-washed cottages clustered about a church spire. High up on the ridge a farmer's deep-mouthed hound was cold trailing the long afternoon away.

I was recalled to consciousness by vaguely noticing hounds drifting off in groups of twos and threes. Reluctantly I arose and called them to me. I put my companion up and we started our long ride home. They said it was twenty-one miles back to the Kennels. Hounds had reached that comfortable degree of sobriety where stray cats and house dogs cease to be of interest and so come comfortably along. The back country was peaceful and of spectral quiet after the turmoil of so long and hard a gallop; the lengthening years have never dimmed the beauty of that ride. We traversed countless country lanes ankle deep in fallen leaves where horses' feet made pleasant rustlings, and long maple-edged avenues into which red and golden leaves were ever filtering. I seemed unconscious of saddle or distance, for truly my fates were busily weaving that which no man may ever entirely cast off. Until then I had been so engrossed in myself and in games and sport that I knew naught of the heart. I knew now, however, that I was very much in love.

We rode on for some time in understanding silence and I was glad, for I knew not what to say that would not have sounded inconsequential. I had my first lesson that day in the eloquence of silence, and learned that conversation is strangled by chatter.

Then, in response to a question she told me of her home in Paris, and of a diminutive Warwickshire cottage where she stayed during the hunting seasons, and we drifted on to favorite authors, to stories that we often re-read, to cherished verses, and we revisited quaint niches and corners of the Old World.

We came at last to a crossroad and asked a country girl to direct us. As we moved on, my companion said, "I once lost my way while hunting in France, and stood at a crossroad just as we have done. A little French child came by and without looking to right or left made me a prim little curtsy and started to pass on. I asked my way, gave her a small coin for directing me, and, being curious, asked her what she would do with it. She looked down at the ground, made a little pile of white dust with her bare toes, looked up at me very solemnly, and said, 'A part for the Mother of Jesus, a part for my own mother,' and then with just the semblance of a smile, 'something good for me,' and walked on." How strange it is, Pendleton, that after so many years her simple little stories should linger on in my memory.

When we reached Lesser Windover we stopped to gaze at its diminutive cemetery, a quiet, peaceful place surrounded by a low gray wall. Years ago some country person of imagination had planted a fringe of cedars along the north which had grown into a feathery reredos. While looking at it she said,

"Do you remember how gay the flowers are in Swiss cemeteries? I once climbed a hillside there to look at a particularly charming little walled cemetery, and said to an old guide who was making hay close by, 'There are more flowers in your cemeteries in Switzerland than in any I have ever seen, and they're wonderfully bright and full of color. Your people must spend much time and work to make them so beautiful.'

"Putting down his scythe he leaned over the wall with me and, gazing at the flowers and simple white stones, said, 'It is because of them that we are here, and Mademoiselle, surely you must know that to be here in Switzerland is good. That is why so many flowers.' He went back to his hay-making and I to my carriage."

On Athelling Hill we turned our horses to look at the lights flickering in the cottages of Afton Village below us and saw the evening star in the east. She asked me where we were and I said, "On the crest of Athelling Hill."

She sat with her hands folded on her knee, the reins hanging loose on the mare's neck. As we turned from looking at the star our eyes met and I reached forward and took her hand, and we gazed off over the great stretches of darkening country, while the hounds stood patiently around us in a circle.

On the far side of the road stood the gaunt ruins of a Revolutionary house with its crumbling chimneys silhouetted against the deepening sky. We could see the outlines of sheep grazing in and around the ruins, and out of the stillness I heard a soft and beautifully modulated voice saying:

"When the quiet colored end of evening smiles
  miles and miles
On the solitary pastures where our sheep
  half asleep
Tinkle homeward through the twilight, stray or stop
  as they crop
Was the site once of a city great and gay,
  (So they say.)"

She did not finish it, and I asked her if she remembered Browning's last verse, and the concluding line; she said yes, commenced to recite it, and then hesitated and said, "Isn't it your turn? Isn't that a man's verse?" So I continued:

"In one year they sent a million fighters forth
  South and North,
And they built their gods a brazen pillar high
  as the sky.
Yet reserved a thousand chariots in full force —
  gold, of course.
Oh heart! Oh blood that freezes, blood that burns!
  earth's return
For whole centuries of folly, noise and sin!
  Shut them in,
With their triumphs and their glories and the rest!
  love is best.

"Do you think it is?" I asked. "I know it is," she answered.
  She looked at her imprisoned hand and then up at me and said, "I'm terribly tired and it's quieting and comforting to have you hold it. There are times when the beauty of outdoors

seems more than one can stand. We have had the sparkle of midday, the glory of sunset, the twilight, and now the evening star and," she hesitated,—"Browning. I don't believe we know what days like this do to us. I have crossed the best countries of England and Ireland, but never had such adventures as we have had. I have thought of you as my knight of old piloting me on and on to the far fringes of the horizon, and to a kill at the world's end. Perhaps the big fence took something out of me, for it was such a hopeless place, and my poor little mare seemed so unequal to it. Will you ever forget being down in the water and looking up at those bleak unfeeling boards?"

Eight o'clock was striking as we rode through Oldfield and turned into the lane that led to the Kennels. I helped her down and saw her to her waiting carriage and said goodnight. As I moved away she called me back, and I thought her voice had a catch in it. When I reached the carriage she said, "Oh, never mind, it's nothing. Thank you, Good-night again and good-bye," and turned her head away.

I surrendered the hounds to Will Simpson, the huntsman, told him briefly of the day, saw our overtired horses done up for the night and, cold and hungry as I was, I sat some time on the club porch fearing any interruption to my thoughts.

When I telephoned her hostess the next afternoon they said she had sailed that morning for her home in Paris.

I followed her to urge my suit. When I reached Paris they said she had gone to Capri. There they told me she had gone to Rome. On my way up to Rome, I read the announcement of her engagement to the Marquis of Oldwick.

I have never seen her, nor until today, even a picture of her, since I helped her to dismount that night at the Kennels.

The Colonel handed me the magazine and I looked at the portrait of a wistfully beautiful woman in a black velvet gown. She had snow white hair. "Eleanor, Marchioness of Oldwick."

CHAPTER XV.

The Last Picture

THE tide of my affairs has turned to the ebb since the events pictured in these stories were enacted, and I have sought a quiet port on one of the "necks" of the Eastern Shore of Maryland. I live in a genial if modest brick house with Revolutionary memories and an old time garden in the care of which I find myself spending more and more time.

Life is exceedingly pleasant in this peaceful back eddy of civilization. I do a bit of informal hunting with our slow, patient, deep voiced Eastern Shore hounds, have an occasional day's shooting, and my garden holds me to eternal vigilance. Best of all are my many kindly neighbors. There are no hunt balls, cup races, or continual comings and goings, nor is my house forever full of people as of yore, but I read more, think more, and on the whole am well content.

Shortly after I moved from my old home, Colonel Weatherford succumbed to a desire of long standing and went to England to live. He had spent much time there, had many friends abroad, and those with whom he was associated in his archaeological work made their headquarters in London.

Through dint of long and consistent frugality I saved enough money to permit my spending last June in England, a project which had its inception in my desire to visit once again with the Colonel.

I refrained from writing him of my plans lest I should interfere with his own arrangements, but shortly after landing I wrote him that I was in England and of my wish to see him. To my everlasting regret I received a note from his secretary to the effect that the Colonel had been ordered away from England by his physician, and would be gone for a month or more, but if I were in the neighborhood would I not come to see his house and garden. The Colonel would want me to see them.

I disembarked from the train one afternoon at the village of Loneminster where I was met by the Colonel's French chauffeur, Eugène, behind whom I had motored winter and summer, in daylight and darkness all up and down the Atlantic seaboard — to quail fields in the Carolinas, duck shooting in Maryland, foxhunting in Virginia and salmon fishing in Canada. I would have given a very great deal to have been back in the cumbersome old Lancaster car sitting beside its owner and starting on one of our earlier sporting adventures. I wonder if the sum total of pleasure one derives from such memories outweighs the regrets for things passed? At the end of a four mile drive we came to the Colonel's English home, an exquisite cottage with a garden upon which time and thought had been lavished. The place was on a diminutive scale, yet ample for one's needs.

At tea time I dispatched a maid to find Albert, in order to learn from him as much as I could about my old friend — what he did, how he spent his days, whether he seemed happy and contented, and what if any were his plans for the future. The picture as it was unfolded gave me good cheer.

THE LAST PICTURE

The Colonel appeared to be on the best of terms with the neighboring gentry and villagers. He had judged the puppies belonging to the local hunt when they had come in from a walk. He had awarded the premiums at the annual flower show — an invitation, according to Albert, that had pleased him more than any he had ever received, and had thrown him into a state of excitement. He had judged hunters at three nearby horse shows, and in March officiated at the hunt steeplechase. His own stable consisted of but one hack which he rode for an hour in the mornings.

According to Albert he read a great deal, spent considerable time on a book he was writing, and often played bridge of an evening with a Sir Henry Furbish, a Professor Saunders, and the Rector, whom Albert had heard him say were the best players in the neighborhood.

Albert was called to take a telephone message, and while he was away I sat enjoying the beauty of the place. The cottage fronted or rather backed on a country lane. The portion of the building which faced the lane was given over to service. The living quarters were in the rear and opened upon a grass terrace. At the foot of the terrace and reached by four broad stone steps was the walled flower garden. Across the garden and on an axis with the center door of the cottage an iron gate of delicate tracery stood open and through it I saw a narrow stream crossed by an old stone bridge covered with moss and ivy. Beyond the bridge was a broad grass covered alley lined with beech hedging, and at the end of the alley one could see the turrets of a stone house.

Had I been in search of a picture to serve me for all time as a symbol of the peace and beauty and security of rural England I would have ended my search at the Colonel's garden, for it seemed to me I was looking at England's heart.

The ominous clouds of depression, war debts, unemployment and exorbitant taxes may float low in the sky, and at times hang motionless, thought I; but I have seen thunder clouds do as much, yet they have always passed over, and the beech hedge and the ivy covered bridge and the beauty of England have remained. The present clouds, I thought, dark as they seem, will leave the beauty of England unmarred.

When Albert returned I asked him who lived in the stone house. "That," said Albert, "is where the dowager Marquise of Oldwick lives." "Oh," I said, and an old memory was awakened. "Her ladyship is an invalid now," continued Albert, "and has to be wheeled about. Do you see where the elm tree casts a shadow, Sir? Well, they bring her ladyship out there every afternoon at tea time and the Colonel goes across the bridge to tea. He will never make any other engagement for that hour. He very often reads to her, and sometimes when the weather is very fine they drive about the park in the pony chaise."

"I don't know how it is, Sir, yet I'm sure the Colonel would not mind me repeating it to you, but as he was going away he said to me, 'Albert, we have been together fifty years, and life has never seemed as precious as it does now. I hope I'm not on the verge of losing it. I wouldn't have minded leaving it any time these last fifty years, but I don't want to leave it now'."

"It's fine isn't it, Sir, that he is so happy now. You wouldn't believe it but I think he's been mostly lonesome all these years. He thought a powerful lot of you, Sir, and if I might say so I think it was your moving away that finally decided him to come here. He will take it very hard not seeing you.

I suppose it may be a long time before you get back. There can't be many more long times for the Colonel and me, can there, Sir? Not at our age."

A week later as I sat in my deck chair reviewing my trip to England I conjured up a happy picture of my old friend. I saw him doing his bit at all the local functions of the countryside; I knew he would be respected by all, and in time affectionately regarded by many, but above all my mind kept reverting again and again to the hour of tea time, to the hour when he would pass across his terrace, down the stone steps and over the ivy covered bridge to where a frail, white-haired, and still beautiful woman would await him in her wheeled chair and they would discuss with minds that were ever young the happenings of the day at home and abroad. I saw him reading the newest book to her and now and anon from the English poets. There was nothing sombre or frayed or old in the picture. That the Colonel might be a bit bent, or the lady of his dreams a frail invalid, these things were not of the substance, for, said I, didn't he tell her that night on the crest of Athelling Hill when he was but a boy and she a girl, that love was best; and didn't she answer that she knew it was? This is the picture I brought home with me to my Eastern Shore of Maryland. My last picture of John Weatherford, sportsman.

THE END